MW01611169

Inc—... at Exeter Depot

~ A Maryvonne Mini-Mystery: ~
By RM Allen

At the Heavenly Depot funeral home,
a casket opens…and poof, the body is gone!
Who snatched it? Where does it end up?

Join artist-sleuth Maryvonne as she sifts through some of
the creepiest lore in town. Meet noted Exeter suffragist
Kate H. Davis and her High Street feminist friends in
1903, as well as Black entrepreneur and host to many US
presidents, John Garrison Cutler. A fun way to learn about
the Suffragist era communities, both black and white,
in Exeter, New Hampshire.

Exeter Green Press | Exeter, New Hampshire
2021

Exeter Green Press
Exeter, New Hampshire
...
ISBN-13: 978-0-9883744-4-7

In memory of Exeter's Golden Girls:
Dr. Alice Chesley 1861-1943
Katherine H. Davis 1847-1926
Annie L. Davis 1869-1933
Ella Follansby 1846-1907

Dedicated to
Rebecca (Barbadoes) Walker (1860-1922)
and mothers and children everywhere…

Special thanks to:
Exeter Historical Society
Lew Hitzrot
David Kruger
David Weber

Old Historical Facts

- John Garrison Cutler 1833-1913 *(above)*
- Cutler's Sea View Hotel existed as described, burned in 1985
- Cutler's restaurant still stands, now Ron's Landing at Hampton Beach. Cutler Ave ran to rear of complex
- Rebecca E. and Ethel Walker are Robinson's alumna
- Kate, Anne, Ella, and Alice all lived on High Street, Exeter
- A State-wide referendum on Women's Suffrage was held on March 10, 1903. Exeter's men voted: 103 yes, and 109 no.
- The Exeter Cemetery includes the graves of the High Street girls, all off the "Main St." J.G. Cutler is buried in Hampton
- The Walker family is buried in plot 1301 at the Exeter Cemetery. One military-issue headstone for Phillip.

New Historical Facts

- Cutler's building at 127 Water Street now has a marker
- Inquiry into Rebecca Walker stone at plot 1301
- Robinson Female Seminary Trustees obtain tax and slave records of William Robinson in 2020
- First public info-session on Black Heritage Pocket-Park proposal held online via Zoom in February 2021

CONTENTS

(Song titles associated with the great Black divas of the disco era: Donna Summer, Gloria Gaynor, Anita Ward, Diana Ross, Thelma Houston, and Evelyn "Champagne" King)

Chapter 1

I'm Coming Out

The vintage gilt casket clicked its way slowly along the track at the Heavenly Depot funeral home. It slid slowly from behind a red velvet curtain at the side of the crowded room. Inch by inch, it crept past the mural on the cracked wall behind, casting its bulky shadow on faded impressions of mountains, lakes, and bucolic countryside scenes.

Outside the funeral home, which was directly adjacent to the real Exeter Depot, the 10:15 had just arrived to the station with a vigorous blasting of its air horn. That had been the signal to start the casket along the tracks inside the funeral home. The real sound effects were part of the schtick of the Heavenly Depot, and had been for nearly one hundred years.

The shriveled body of ninety-two-year-old Albere Hone Lyman, known to all as "Honey," was to make his final journey inside this closed casket. The owner of the funeral home, Clive Junkins, another man in his ninety-second year, stood in his conductor's cap operating the track controls at the base of the antique stage at the front of the room.

Clive had performed this ritual many times over his long career. Today, he looked slightly weepy as he awaited the arrival of the creeping casket to the small turntable in the center of the crowd.

On the stage stood the man who would be master of ceremonies this morning, Honey's mentee and good friend, Jefferson Ream.

The click, click, click was mesmerizing and left plenty of time for reflection on one's own mortality.

The 1928-era room with its tiny, creaking wooden seats was beginning to get uncomfortably steamy this late March morning from all the live bodies pressing in to get a view of Honey's final scene. Maryvonne was overheating and pulled off her scarf for some relief, inadvertently dropping it to the floor, where she was momentarily

1

distracted by all the footwear - especially those grey shoes with the black laces worn by the man seated in front of her.

"Oh la la," she said under her breath, wanting to get a good look at his face before the end of the ceremony.

Because she had been thus distracted, when she sat back up, she noticed that everyone in the room was entranced by the slow-motion journey of the casket, which was finally nearing the turntable. The casket acted as a magnet, turning all heads slowly in its direction.

Maryvonne's glance swept the room, amused at the curious sight of this room from another era and the seemingly hypnotized mourners. Toward the back of the room she noticed a professional cameraman getting comfortable in a perch up in the rear catwalk, capturing the scene for the benefit of posterity.

A loud click and the sound of well-oiled metal latches sliding into place had the same magnetic effect on Maryvonne, coaxing her eyes back toward the now arrived casket. The turntable softly lit up from underneath, causing the gilt ornamenture of the casket to glow. The crowd gawked at this spectacle, and let out a hushed, "Oooo." A slightly perceptible sound of clanking gears was all that could be heard as Clive pulled some levers and the old turntable rotated the casket so that it was now headed directly towards the stage.

Then, whooshing hydraulics accompanied a slight tilting of the turntable by about ten inches, so the head of the casket was raised skyward to meet the shining tracks that rose up a small incline to the stage. The casket was stilled, all eyes were upon it. Clive pushed a button and inside the room a long and loud train whistled blasted out, vibrating the walls and startling the crowd - causing them to giggle nervously. He yelled out in his croaking voice: "All aboard!"

2

Click, click, click – the coffin began to ascend toward the stage, which was painted with a sunny blue-sky background, dotted with heavenly clouds. A small section in the center of the wall was covered with powder blue velvet curtains, and the shiny tracks ran directly into it. Honey was on track to pass directly into heaven. But first he would stop alongside Jefferson, who shuffled his notes nervously as the casket kept rising before him.

The gleaming casket was just now passing by Honey's only family member in attendance, his great-niece Audrey. Maryvonne noticed she put her hands over her heart while the casket passed by her at eye level.

The clicking casket was tilted in such a way that the mourners could see that the lid of the casket was in two sections; the smaller of the two sections was near the head. Click, click, click click…then nothing. The casket seemed to have stopped just slightly short of the stage, appearing to be stuck.

Clive yanked strenuously on the levers a few times, and the casket jerked, causing the mourners to cringe and squirm, then it continued its curious rise to center stage as Clive began dinging a small bell.

Jefferson settled his papers and cleared his throat as the casket stopped alongside him. He turned and looked forlornly at the fancy box beside him and said, "Goodbye, Honey."

Suddenly, a flash; and an explosion that blasted the small door of the coffin open as copious amounts of smoke billowed out. Jefferson jumped back, gripping his papers to his chest and running off backstage. People screamed and chairs were overturned. Clive stood gaping with his conductor's cap askew.

Clive's son, seated in the first row close by to his elderly dad, ran up on the stage to put out the fire. Only there was not any fire. He fanned the smoke away, and the slightly charred inside of the coffin came into view, and…

3

no Honey. Once the crowd recognized this, the screaming started anew.

"Dear Jesus, his head was blasted off!" one heavy-set woman wailed.

"Where the hell is it?" yelled someone else, causing more confusion as squealing people looked under the chairs near them.

From the stage came a loud voice. "Calm down, everyone, his head is not blown off. As a matter of fact, he is not even in the box," said Clive's son, also named Clive, standing beside the smoking coffin with an incredulous look on his face. Great-niece Audrey stood up quickly, white as a ghost. The crowd began to chatter.

"In the name of all that is holy, what is going on here?" demanded the school principal.

"This is crazy, I'm getting out of here. Feels like there is a curse or something. Damn creepy place," said a middle-aged man who grabbed his stunned wife by the arm and headed for the crowded exit.

Many of the people, including Audrey guided by her boyfriend, made a bee-line for the now-open doors.

Old Clive, still at the controls, was quite close to Maryvonne. He spoke aloud, mostly to himself, "That son of a bitch, he just had to have the last laugh." Maryvonne was still stuck to her chair, slightly paralyzed by the shock, but she heard him through her daze. She stood up and went over to old Clive.

"Are you okay, Clive? Can I get you a seat?" She didn't wait for an answer, but pulled a chair close to him so he could sit down.

Clive sat with a thud, and took off his crooked cap. For a brief moment his eyes darted back and forth in their sockets, then he burst out laughing. He laughed and laughed and laughed. He laughed himself into a coughing fit and began choking to catch his breath. His son Clive quickly ran down the small side steps of the stage and came to his father's side. Old man Clive finally caught his breath, then wheezed and started laughing again.

"What the devil has gotten into you, Pop?" exclaimed the bewildered son.

"Oh, I bet my hat that ole' Honey orchestrated this somehow. A showman to the last. Let's go out back and find his wretched body; it has to be there somewhere."

"You can't be serious, Pop."

"Dead serious, me boy. Make an announcement and calm the crowd. Tell 'em we'll be right back."

Clive the younger jumped back on the stage to take control of the situation. Clive the elder asked Maryvonne to help him get out back to the workrooms and the family room to investigate.

Maryvonne held the nonagenarian by the arm as he began walking unsteadily towards the non-public area of the old funeral home. They were quickly joined by Clive the younger in the back rooms. Maryvonne clung onto her ward as they went from room to room, looking for the body. Nothing. In the last room, the embalming area, Clive the elder came to his senses and got very sober.

"This is not good. Not good at all. Perhaps it's not a joke."

"I didn't think so, Pop. We're going to have to call the police and report a missing body."

"Jesus, Mary, and Joseph. The end is nigh. Okay, I'll make the call," sighed the old man. "You go out and tell the folks show's over and clear out the building."

The younger Clive sped off. Maryvonne helped the old man into a seat by the desk phone in the prep room area. Resigned, he dialed and waited. Maryvonne heard the hello on the other end. "Harry? This is Clive. Uhhh, we have a situation at the Heavenly Depot, can you come on over and…"

Maryvonne didn't hear the rest of the call. She had never been in an embalming area and was fascinated. She

5

looked around, slightly horrified, taking it all in. She became aware that Clive was calling her name and rapping a cane against the desk.

"Maryvonne…Maryvonne! Earth to Maryvonne."

"Oh, sorry, Clive. I didn't hear you. I'm pretty freaked out about poor Honey, and then this room. Mon Dieu! I can't believe any of this."

"I can't either. What happened to him is beyond me. Just yesterday I had him all wrapped up like he asked. He wanted to be wrapped up like an Egyptian mummy in golden silk cloth. Can you imagine?" He gestured over to a pile of honey-gold silk strips on a table. Maryvonne visibly shuddered.

"My son and I worked on him all day, embalmed him like King Tut and wrapped him up as he requested, then strapped him in the Casket Caboose last night and went home. What'd Honey do – rise from the dead and walk away?" Clive drummed his fingers on a metal table with wheels as he stewed on his thoughts. "Couldn't be. Impossible." Clive drummed his gnarled fingers some more, causing an echo in the tiled room.

Maryvonne shivered again, getting more creeped out by the minute. The door finally opened and Clive's son appeared.

Maryvonne interrupted, "I'm sorry, Clive, but I am going to have to go now and get some fresh air. This day has been too much. You two will be okay? I hear the police coming now. So, let me just get out of the way." And with that, she hurriedly left the embalming room by a back door and walked around to the front.

~ ~ ~

A knot of the frenetic fray of people leaving the parking lot stopped her in her tracks. She could see the police cruiser was trying to enter the chaotic parking lot.

6

Cars were jamming the exit, and people were talking excitedly in small groups on the sidewalks beyond.

Maryvonne decided it was best to leave her car in the lot until it cleared out some. Beside her was the garden area in front of the Heavenly Depot and she could see the roof of Gerry's Trackside Variety in the distance at the far end of the real train station's parking lot. She decided to cut through the garden to Gerry's to get a hot cup of coffee and a grip on herself.

On her tiptoes, so as to not get her spike heels dirty in the muddy grass, she passed by a small, ornate replica of a turntable in the center of the garden which made her shudder once again. She slipped through a jagged opening in the chain link fence that separated the Heavenly Depot property from the real Exeter Train Station, a stop on the Amtrak's Downeaster line, running from Boston to Portland, Maine.

In the parking lot of the train station, she passed by the cameraman. He was holding a bunch of equipment and talking to a couple of younger guys near their car. As they got into the car, she heard them making macabre jokes and reliving the experience. She walked faster and faster, not because of the chilly spring air, but so she wouldn't have to hear them.

At the back of a variety store was a small breakfast diner. She saw an open stool at the old Formica counter, sat down and ordered a cup of coffee; black and strong. The blonde waitress poured one out and slid it over to her. Maryvonne held on to it for dear life, warming her trembling hands.

What on earth had she just witnessed? Where was Honey? Poor, dear. Honey. She had been very fond of the old man.

Maryvonne was an artist and she knew Honey from the local art scene. In his long retirement, Honey did small performance pieces on occasion for the town art shows put on by the Arts & Culture Committee. The painters and performers all attended the art openings where they fraternized with each other, as well as customers, while sipping wine.

Maryvonne brushed her long blonde bangs out of her eyes, leaned her nose in, took a dramatic whiff of the very hot coffee, and then blew on it to hasten the cooling. The earthy aroma of the coffee made her begin to feel more settled. She thought about Honey some more and her green eyes smiled. She remembered that when she first met him, he was over seventy and doing his thing at a small Avant Garde art show out of town entitled "Binders of Women."

The show was in response to a foolish comment made by a politician of the times. Honey had set up a booth in the corner of the show, where he was dressed as a politician carrying a briefcase emblazoned with the phrase "Women-Binders."

To any woman passing by, he offered to tightly bind her feet with large strips of panty hose. Maryvonne, a shoe freak of the first order, took the bait. She sat down, took off her Steve Madden snakeskin loafers and raised a dainty foot. Honey then introduced himself, bound her feet in a grandiose fashion, and took a Polaroid photo which he then tacked to the wall.

She liked him at once and they had been friends ever since. He had really slowed down over the past few years, and she had not seen him at any recent shows, but she did see him at Joe Saints coffee shop a few times.

She tentatively sipped her coffee and thought about the last time she had seen him there. The two of them made an odd pair. She a voluptuous blond in her fifties, and he a tiny, pale, man with good hair - in his nineties - sharing stories over coffee at Joe Saints across town, laughing loudly and freely. They had that in common; big, easy smiles and hearty laughs. Honey had

8

told her about a Roman birthday party he threw for himself back before he was head of the drama department at the local prep school.

A dedicated lover and patron of the arts, Honey had hired a curvaceous female model to lie on her side on a large board, nude. She was then artfully draped, and surrounded by appetizers like grapes, strawberries, cheese, and iced shrimp. Men in togas carried the bountiful board through the party for the faculty guests to snack from. How he laughed when telling her about the hell he had to pay to the school admin when they found out about his antics, and how it almost held back his promotion to department chair.

Maryvonne chuckled a little now, remembering how hilarious their discussion had been then. She had called him a 1970's misogynist, and he had retorted by trying to call her the opposite. Only he couldn't remember the word "misandrist," and had said "mis-husbandrist." She took a long swallow of the hot coffee. Poor Honey, where was he now?

She hoped the police would figure it out quickly and all would be well when she went back to get her car. How could it be otherwise? Who would want to steal his body anyway? He didn't appear to have any enemies. He didn't seem wealthy. Honey was a confirmed bachelor of the old-school type, who had outlived most of his relatives and peers. It didn't make sense.

Maryvonne sipped her coffee and gazed at the footwear of the other patrons whose legs dangled off the old silver stools. Mostly workboots.

Cup empty, she left a few dollars on the counter and headed out the door to retrieve her car. It was chilly outside and she pulled the scarf from her coat pocket and wrapped it around her neck again. The last few dregs of grey, crusted snow clung on in shadowed corners of the neighborhood. Maryvonne eyed them with contempt, for she was a summer-lover.

But April was just days away, and the weather forecast was on the upswing. Soon enough, the summer wind would come a-blowing in and she would be able to put the top down in her husband's blue Miata, affectionately known as the Zeus-Mobile.

Keeping to the sidewalk this time, she came to the entrance of the parking lot, and only a few cars remained. The police were stringing yellow crime scene tape around the funeral home. It was apparent to her that the situation was not over yet. Maryvonne's little electric Ford was parked away from all that, just off the sidewalk, so she quickly got in and left them undisturbed to do their work.

Silently she drove the car the two miles home, through the bustling village center with its old statue of Lady Justice atop the brick town hall. Up the hill of High Street, past the two towered homes across from each other that flanked the street near the hospital, and finally, into her driveway.

~~~

Entering the sanctuary of her home, she pulled the door shut behind her and called for her husband. "Zeus! Mon chéri! Where are you?" His muffled reply floated up from his wood shop in the cellar. Maryvonne didn't even take her coat off before running down the stairs to talk to him.

"How was the funeral?" Zeus asked, his blue eyes looking up from the table saw, wood dust settled in uneven spots in his silver curls.

Maryvonne's full French heritage was on display as she made a rapid sign of the cross upon herself while saying a portion of the Hail Mary prayer in French, ending with "mort, mort, mort...NO!"

"Hold on! What happened?" He switched off the whizzing saw and in the quiet of the dusty, cobwebby, grey cellar she told him all.

He interrupted occasionally to incredulously remark on the absurdity of what she was relating: "Wrapped like a golden mummy?... Smoke coming out of a coffin?... The police are cordoning off the funeral home?" When she was done, he was silent, and just stared at her.

"Mon chéri, why are you so quiet?" she asked apprehensively.

He glanced past her, "Shhh. There is something big and dark coming up behind you..."

Then he roared "I think it is a zombie!" and grabbed her and pulled her in tight to his chest while she screamed and tried to beat him with her fists.

"Diaboltin du Satan! You imp! This is serious," she protested.

"I'm serious too: there is a golden-mummy-Zombie on the loose and I must protect my woman."

"Sometimes you are just like a small child, mon chéri," she admonished. "But you do know how to make me laugh!" and she kissed him on the cheek. "Thanks for lightening my mood some. I'm going upstairs to take off my coat and these heels now."

"Sorry for being irreverent about Honey. It's a tragedy for sure, but I am sure the police will figure it out. Wait for me - I'm coming too. Just let me get this box for the junk piles. I finally weeded out my collection." He went to a dark corner and picked up a cardboard box full of broken model airplane parts and bits from the seventies.

"Glad to see you doing some spring cleaning down here," she congratulated him, wrinkling her nose. "Just put it near that other junk I piled in the garage and I will work it all into a couple of blue bags for trash day. I'll sort through all that stuff, to see what needs to go in the

11

recycle bin or be donated to the thrift shop before we get rid of it."

Up in the bedroom, she finally took off the Nine West black patent spike heels she had been tottering around in all morning and put them in the closet. Zeus came in at that moment and said, "Looks like you could weed out some of your collection too."

"Never!" she snorted. "They are my babies," she cooed, picking up a purple suede mid-heel and caressing it. She set it back down beside a grey pump with a slim, black stacked heel and stood up suddenly and exclaimed, "Oh la la!" She had suddenly remembered about the man with the grey shoes seated in front of her. She had never gotten to see his face in all the confusion.

"What now?" inquired her long-suffering husband.

"At the funeral, there was a man sitting in front of me. I recognized him from the back, and by his grey shoes with the black laces."

"So?"

"I don't know who he is, but I have seen him a few times at the train station, when I am there endlessly trainspotting with little Charlie."

"So?"

"I've seen him maybe about three times in six months or so. He comes at different times and on different days, and it is always the same thing. I don't think he notices me, but I watch him from afar. He waits on the platform, and when the train arrives, he leaves."

"So? Isn't that the same thing you do with your grandson?"

"Well, yes. I'll admit that. But this guy is not three years old like little Charlie. And we are not always on the platform. Sometimes we are down at the gates, sometimes near the baggage house, or on the tiny turntable in the garden. Sometimes way down the line on the old train bridge. We could be anywhere. Charlie is obsessed with looking at all the parts of the train from different angles. But this guy, the handful of times I've seen him there, is always on the platform."

"And…?"

"What is he doing? I'm thinking it is nefarious in some way. It's just not normal behavior for a grown man."

"Did you ask him about this at the funeral?"

"No, things went crazy and I forgot all about it. Plus, what would I say? To satisfy my idle curiosity, I just wanted to look into his face and see whatever is there. Too bad. Well, I have one clue anyway to this mystery; he knew Honey Lyman."

"Are you working on a mystery? Oh no! I remember your last two mysteries. Are you becoming a professional sleuth now?"

In the last two years Maryvonne had solved, but not solved, two incidents that happened in town. In one, she had figured out who had lifted a rare document before anyone really knew it was even stolen. In the other, her uncle had gone missing during a hurricane and she was the one to rescue him. In both incidents, she had had help from spirits of the past. But she pretty much kept that part to herself.

"Of course not, don't be silly. I just noticed something odd, I'm not going to do anything about it."

"Sure, you aren't. I really hope you don't, Maryvonne. Really."

Chapter 2

Upside Down

Jefferson Reed had promised his mentor and good friend Honey Lyman that he would be the master of ceremonies at his funeral. This he had promised twenty years ago upon Honey's long over-due retirement from the drama department. It was now Jefferson's time to retire, and he did not need this.

Back when he and Honey originally agreed upon this, it seemed a simple matter. But over the years it grew into what had now turned out to be a monster. Honey wanted a dramatic final scene. Okay. Then it became the scene to end all parting scenes. Okay. Then it became something that seemed to be, perhaps, illegal?

"Jeff, it's nothing. After it's all over, wheel me out on the stage on a gurney. I'll be all wrapped up like a mummy. Just wheel me out and show me to the people. They'll love it. They know that's how I am. It'll be a gas. I can't wait to see ol' Clive's face." That is exactly what Honey had said.

Now Jeff sat in his house alone. He had intentionally left his cell phone in the car. But he knew it would only be a matter of time.

Should he come clean? Best not. He had no idea what had happened. Honey had to turn up somewhere.

Perhaps Honey had turned the whole thing upside down, and the joke was actually intended to be on *him*? He and Honey had pulled a lot of theatrical stunts over the years, but this took the cake. Would Honey actually do this to him? They were great friends, after all. It just didn't make sense.

But…. but there was that part of Honey's life that he kept very private. All Jeff knew was that every year he took off for a couple of months to go to New York and watch all the new Broadway productions. At least that is what he said. And he seemed to be able to talk about the shows in detail, so Jeff never questioned it.

16

Now that he thought about it, he wondered why Honey never talked about where he stayed, or who he was with in the city. Jeff had never met any of his relatives, save the one great-niece, Audrey.

Audrey had come to live in Exeter about five years ago. She was markedly different in temperament from her great uncle. He was the gregarious man-about-town, she the quiet homemaker. Well, not really, she didn't have any children of her own, but she did work long hours at that curtain shop by the train station and had an on-again-off-again boyfriend that hung about.

Shortly before Audrey moved from New York to Exeter, Honey up and sold his house and moved to the big retirement community in the woods on the edge of Exeter, Bubbling Brook. Jeff had wondered at the time how Honey could afford to live there; he had always taken him as a man of moderate means.

Jeff had asked him about it, and Honey just brushed him off in his usual manner - diverting his attention quickly to another topic he contagiously enthused about. Honey was indeed very deft when he played the gadfly, and always did have more than his share of energy.

At this point, Jeff had to ask himself: was Honey really dead?

~~~

The police were wrapping up for the day at the Heavenly Depot funeral home, and the Clives were glad. Old man Clive seemed physically very tired, and his son was even more tired of the entire affair.

Clive the younger, actually Clive Junkins the third -called CJ by his family and friends- had wanted his dad to close down the old funeral home decades ago. CJ thought it was a relic of the past, and in actuality, was embarrassed

17

by it. But old Clive had inherited it from his father, the original Clive -also known as Grampa Clive- and was devoted to it.

Grampa Clive had purchased the old turntable and engine house adjacent to the Exeter Depot from the railroad when it was decommissioned in 1922, as automobiles began to take over, and turned it into the Heavenly Depot funeral home shortly thereafter.

The large turntable area in front was converted into a garden with a small turntable replica as the centerpiece, and the four-bay engine house was converted into a funeral parlor. One half became the public parlor with tracks and stage, and the other half was divided into three smaller rooms: a morgue, a prep room and office area, and a private family viewing room. The private family viewing room was where the Casket Caboose was placed on the tracks to begin the journey through the red velvet curtains, past the countryside, and up into the puffy clouds of heaven.

The venture had been a huge hit. At-home funerals were just going out of fashion in favor of professional funeral parlors, and Grampa Clive rode the wave. It was very profitable, to say the least. It did take a hit during the Great Depression, but managed to bounce back nicely. The heyday of the place was in the nineteen fifties and sixties. Grampa Clive made a bundle, which he put in the stock market.

Old Clive took it over in the early seventies, but by then, the US craze in railroad funerals was petering out. He had owned it for nearly fifty years now, just barely eking out a profit from it. But he kept it for the love of railroading. Grampa Clive had invested wisely in bank and railroad stocks, and those came to Old Clive in a trust fund in the seventies as well, enabling him to keep the old Heavenly Depot in reasonable shape. That fund was all but depleted ten years ago, but for some reason CJ could not convince Old Clive to sell.

Old Clive's second love, behind railroading, was gardening, and after his wife died, he spent even more time puttering in the Heavenly Depot garden. The result was gorgeous, and mothers would often bring their small children there to take a slow swirl on the tiny turntable. Old Clive loved watching them enjoy the gardens and getting all excited when the new Downeaster would come tooting into the station, which was in perfect view behind the chain-link fence.

CJ followed in the footsteps of the family funeral business, but he worked at another firm across town, Greely's. He earned a mortuary science degree from a fine mortuary school and passed his exams with flying colors. On the job, he did all the usual mortician tasks. He was a natural and performed them with precision, sometimes at Greely's and sometimes in the morgue and prep room at the Heavenly Depot, which was kept in perfect, certified working order. In other words, Greely's rented out the Heavenly Depot work spaces for its overflow. That kept the lights on and the taxes paid for Old Clive.

CJ had finally cornered Old Clive five years ago about selling. Old Clive confessed he too thought the place should close, but he had made a promise. He was keeping it open until his old buddy, Honey Lyman died. "Could be any day now, me boy," Old Clive had said. CJ just groaned.

That long-delayed day had finally come.

CJ pulled on his mustache, which is what he tended to do when stressed. He just wanted to sell the place for cash and be done with it. The building was on its last legs anyway, the parking was more valuable at this point. Greely's could easily contract with another outfit for overflow work, no harm done there. He himself was now nearing retirement and the cash would make a nice nest-

19

egg. CJ figured the cops would shut the place down now, and the old man would finally sell.

After a brief discussion, CJ and Old Clive had been instructed to wait in the private family room while the police secured the scene and began their search for clues. Sargent Henry finally appeared and sat down on the antique red velvet fainting couch.

"So, we have a mummy on the loose in town. And last you saw of him he was in the Casket Caboose this morning. Now to my thinking, mummies don't leave fingerprints on caskets, but people do. Our unit is dusting the work rooms now. I'll send someone in to take your prints, and we will see what else turns up. Who else will we be finding?"

CJ pulled on his moustache and replied, "Well, let's see. There was me and dad here all day yesterday... and then this morning only Honey's great niece, Audrey, and Jefferson Reed came into the family room."

"Maryvonne was in here too, in the workrooms while we searched; she left just before you came in," croaked Old Clive.

"Maryvonne! She does have a knack for being in the action, that one," replied Sargent Henry, raising his eyebrows. "Anyone else?"

"No," replied Old Clive.

"Yes," replied CJ. "Miguel from Greely's delivered Honey three days ago. He pushed the gurney right in through the rear delivery door, and slid him into a drawer in the morgue. We chatted for a while, then he left and I locked up."

Sargent Henry was jotting all this down. Old Clive shifted in his seat and grasped his cane. "Look here, Henry, I gotta see a man about a horse. Mind if I slip right over there into the toilet before this fingerprint business?"

While Old Clive was relieving his bladder, the police officer went out to speak to his team. CJ sat alone,

20

stroking and tugging his graying moustache. He hoped the police didn't turn the place upside down.

~~~

Audrey Lyman sat with her forehead down on the cutting table, piles of floral curtain fabric littered about. Although she was in her early-thirties, her gamine haircut and smallish figure made her look like a collapsed elf in the meadow.

Richard Bush, her boyfriend, and Sylvia Cole, her best friend, were sitting alongside her and trying to console her.

"It just reminded me of the car accident when I lost my parents, all the fire and the smoke," Audrey said in a very small voice.

"I know, sugar, but it was not. You are safe," Sylvia comforted her. "We're here with you and you are safe." Sylvia picked up Audrey's small, pale hand in her ebony one and patted it. "You are safe."

Audrey raised her head and gave a weak smile. "Thanks," she replied, then sat up fully and sighed, long and loud. Richard continued rubbing her back.

She looked as though she was finally beginning to rally. "Thanks a lot. You guys are wonderfully kind. I guess I just got triggered there. I must have some PTSD still lingering from that accident so many years ago. I miss my parents; my dad always watching the Yankees on the telly, and my mom such a lovely and proper British woman. Sometimes I wish I had not survived the accident. It can be so lonely."

"Well you have us, sugar."

"Yes I do. Thanks for getting me out of there so quickly," Audrey said with genuine gratefulness in her voice.

Richard continued rubbing and said, "You looked like you were going to faint, so I just grabbed you. I thought we could get you over here to the shop and away from all the people. When they figure out what happened, they can come tell us. I'm sure everything will be all right in the end."

This caring circle of friends was in the Curtain Factory, a decrepit building that shared the parking lot with the Heavenly Depot. It was a conglomerate of buildings all jammed together and built into a slope so that the front was markedly higher than the rear. The higher, main part of the building was long and narrow, as it had originally been constructed as a bowling alley at the turn of the century. The rest of the piled-up buildings were filled with winding displays of faux rooms showcasing the latest styles in curtains and upholstery fabrics. People often got disoriented and lost in them.

The three friends were up in the higher section, just inside the front door near the checkout counter. The store was closed on account of the funeral.

"Why don't we go sit on one of the display couches and get you more comfortable? Then I'll make you some tea in the breakroom and bring it over," Richard offered helpfully.

"Yes. Yes, that sounds good," replied Audrey, regaining some of her wits.

She was escorted to the nearest display, a sage green Jacobean affair, accented by cream muslin pillows that sported a bold palm leaf design.

"Would you like to lie back, sugar?" asked Sylvia.

"No, I think I would like to sit up and drink that tea."

Richard was already gone, leaving the two girls holding hands side-by-side on the couch.

"Sylvia, I don't know what came over me in there. I was thinking, Uncle Honey is dead and now I am truly so alone, and then bam! The casket explodes. It was just too much to bear all at once. You must think me a bloody fool for being so barmy."

"Not at all, you can't be married to a psychiatrist and not learn something about PTSD."

"I guess," replied Audrey, looking down at her hands.

"Now look, just because your uncle is gone doesn't mean you are alone. You have got me and my whole family, and Richard too. We need to pry you out of this shop more. You spend too much time tucked away, sewing all alone in a little room."

Audrey did not reply, she just looked away forlornly.

Sylvia tried again, "Look, I don't want to be too pushy, but I want you to come and spend the night at my house tonight. The kids will cheer you up. And when the police find out what happened to your uncle, I'll be right there with you."

Audrey sniffed a little. "That sounds good. I love your kids. I love all kids. I always wanted kids of my own. But I have this fear that I would die in a freak accident and leave them all alone, just like what happened to me. So, I just couldn't...so I never..." she broke off in a choked sob.

Sylvia cradled her and soothed her, repeating, "I'm right here, sugar."

After Audrey was all cried out, she said weakly, "This weird incident is bringing it all back. I think I may need to go see a therapist and just get it out."

"I'm sure my Mark can help you. You can talk to him after supper if you feel up to it."

Audrey heaved a sigh, and put a hand to her head. "Oh, my head is starting to hurt. I think I need some ibuprofen, or maybe the tea will help. What happened to Richard? He seems to be taking a long time."

Audrey looked around for him in vain then continued, "You know, I will stay at your house tonight, and talk to Mark after dinner. I need help; I'm really at loose ends now that Uncle Honey is gone. Where can he possibly be? Oh, Sylvia, it feels like my life is turned upside down, again."

Chapter 3

On the Radio

As the afternoon wore on, Maryvonne was less shaken by the events that morning at the Heavenly Depot. The police had called right away and asked her to come down to their station to make a statement and take her fingerprints, as part of the investigation. She had complied, and as a result felt the whole Honey affair less spine-chilling and more of an actual crime.

The young Officer Bailey Barndollar, with her long brown hair coiled tightly in a bun, had taken her prints and her deposition. During this, Maryvonne had learned that the "explosion" inside the casket was an ordinary theatrical stage prop called a flash-pot, not a bomb or paranormal manifestation of hellfire. This fact had grounded her. Officer Bailey had expressed confidence that the body would turn up one way or another.

Sitting in front of her laptop, Maryvonne decided that a way to stop thinking about the whole grisly affair was to clean out her emails. It had worked. She opened an email that had come the week before from the Exeter LitFest that publicized their schedule, but that she hadn't had a chance to look at.

The town held an annual weekend festival of local and regional authors the first weekend each April. The schedule had been sent out via email last week, and finally Maryvonne had some time to look to see which events she would like to attend this upcoming weekend.

She clicked in and saw the welcome message from the event organizer, Ellen Swartz, who happened to be a good friend of hers. Along with being a superb organizer, Ellen was a fantastic wordsmith, and her message was quite catchy. The annual fest had a theme this year of "Other-Worldly." Perusing the list of names, Maryvonne saw many local authors she knew and enjoyed, for Exeter had more than its fair share of talented local writers.

26

Taking a pencil, she quickly noted the day, time, and venue of the writers she wanted to hear, trying to avoid any conflicts. Maryvonne noted with interest that Lisa Bunker and Alex Myers were to appear together in a panel discussion on early transgender stories.

Reading the description of the panel gave Maryvonne pause. Honey Lyman was still in the back of her mind, and she was suddenly struck with the thought that perhaps Honey was a transgender person?

After all, he was a small man with full hair, and a definite diva of the stage. She had read somewhere that about two percent of people are born with "ambiguous" anatomy. In the past, most hermaphrodites tried hide this fact, but now a days acceptance was asked for. Maybe Honey had never "come out" for Honey was Honey and had always been Honey - so who cared. But that could be one reason why his body was missing, now wouldn't it be? To keep the secret forever?

Still pondering this, Maryvonne saw on the event list the public hours of the literary-themed art show in the town hall that coincided with the LitFest, and added that to her notes. She was really looking forward to viewing that show with her husband.

The "call to artists" had gone out the prior April, so local artists had all year to come up with a piece of artwork on a literary theme; the more local the better. Maryvonne had dropped off her canvas two weeks ago to the Arts & Cultural Committee.

Hers was a self-portrait featuring Tabitha Gilman Tenney's 1801 book, *Female Quixotism*. The book cover took up most of the canvas, and Maryvonne's green eyes and blonde bangs could been seen peeping over the top of the book as she read it. The eyes were the focus, peeping up in an amused fashion through a striking pair of cat-eye glasses. The book, *Female Quixotism,* was hilarious and early feminist and Maryvonne thought she had captured the feeling of it correctly on the canvas.

After clearing out scads of other emails, she felt she had been sitting for long enough and got up and went downstairs. Plus, something was beginning to smell very good. Zeus was in the kitchen boiling chicken bones into a nutritious broth.

"Mmmm, it smells fantastique down here, mon chéri, I do adore a man who can cook," she praised him while the herby scent flowed into her being.

"What about a man who can do something else?" he said as he came up behind her at the bubbling pot and wrapped his strong arms around her, kissing her on the nape of her neck.

"Ah, oui, oui, oui, amore," she giggled. He turned her around to face him.

"Are you feeling better now? You had quite the scare this morning, so I am cooking you a big pot of broth to bolster your health. I'll simmer all day, and tomorrow I will strain it and add the veggies. This could be the last pot of the season, since spring seems to have almost arrived."

"Oui, it's going to be a chilly LitFest this weekend, but thankfully, most of the events are indoors. The pot of soup will do us good though," she observed.

"Do you have the schedule? I'd like to see it," Zeus asked.

"Sure, I will forward it to you and let's see which ones we would like to attend together." She turned back to the bubbling pot and picked up the wooden spoon to give it a stir. "You know, I have been thinking. What if Honey was transgender and hiding it, and that is why the body has gone missing?"

"Are you kidding?' he asked, then noticed she was serious. "Well, that question seems far-fetched. But what it does tell me is that you are getting sucked into this mystery," he replied flatly.

"So, what if I am? Honey was my friend. I would like to help him out," Maryvonne said with compassion.

"By invading his privacy to reveal him as transgender? That's not overly friendly. Plus, I see no reason to question his or anyone else's gender. It's the twenty-first century; let people be who they want to be. Now, what a real detective would do is follow the money. Who stands to gain?" he said pointedly. "Not that I want you to do that," he added quickly.

But it was too late, Maryvonne stopped in mid-stir, cocked her head and furrowed her brow in sleuth-mode like Peter Falk's Columbo. Zeus interrupted, "Now don't do that, it is not your business. Let the police handle it."

"Naturalmente, mon chéri. But I can think about it and come up with my own theories, can't I?" she said primly.

"Like your very thin transgender theory?"

"Perhaps," she replied confidently. "Now if you will excuse me, I'm going into the garage to sort through those piles of junk, and maybe come up with more theories to help poor Honey finally rest in peace." She took a light coat out of the closet and strode past him towards the door of the unheated garage.

"You are a piece of work, Maryvonne," he laughed while turning the boiling pot down low for a long simmer, and returning to his crossword puzzles on the kitchen counter.

Out in the chilly garage, Maryvonne surveyed the outcome of her spring cleaning. A higgledy-piggledy heap. Stuff piled against the wall included: a bag of clothes, a heaping box of kitchen-related items, faded seasonal things atop a pile of old magazines atop a pile of worn-out doormats, and the dusty box of broken model airplanes pushed up against all that. Off to the side waited a large empty rectangular box marked "thrift shop" and a large, blue, wheeled recycle bin. She had a net-zero policy; for any item that came into the house, one had to go out. If they were too bad, they went to a rag bag or the trash, otherwise they got donated.

An old dusty radio hung on the wall on a hook. Maryvonne flicked it on, turned it up, and pulled the bag of clothes toward her to begin the sorting task. A pile of Zeus's tee shirts with disintegrated collars came out of the bag first. She held each item up for inspection and sorting.

On the radio, the host was talking about the origins of disco music. Maryvonne did not know that the music genre had grown partially out of Jazz and Rhythm and Blues and was considered to be Black music by many. She had always thought of it as European. But no, it was actually heavily comprised of Black dance music played in French discos in the seventies.

The radio show host spoke of the old dance show Soul Train, and that brought back many memories. How Maryvonne had loved that television show back then! It was full of the best music and the best dancers, and she would be glued to it. And the shoes! Some of the shoes were outrageously fun.

The host's topic turned to disco divas, and he listed a handful of Black women Maryvonne was very familiar with: Donna Summer, Thelma Houston, Gloria Gaynor, Diana Ross, and Evelyn "Champagne" King. Just by the host saying their names, Maryvonne could begin to feel the driving "four on the floor" beat in her head. Then some syncopated rhythm, a little chicken scratch on the guitar, and before she knew it Maryvonne was shuffling her feet.

"Get to the music!" Maryvonne called out to the radio host, and finally he did. Maryvonne danced like mad on the cement floor, with one of her old sweaters, to Vickie Sue Robinson's *Turn the Beat Around*.

And when the drummer starts beating that beat
He nails that beat with the syncopated rhythm
With the rat, tat, tat, tat, tat, tat on the drums, hey
Turn the beat around
Love to hear percussion

She danced with various articles of clothing, and did the Bump with the wheeled recycle bin. She danced until she was out of breath. The radio continued playing killer dance songs, and Maryvonne continued sorting and dancing. The dancing made her melancholy mood begin to clear. She went through the clothes bag, then moved onto the kitchen items, sorting into the correct piles.

Donna Summer's hit song *On the Radio* began as she tackled the box of old airplanes. Some of the bits were recyclable, so she put some in the blue bin, and then crushed and stuffed others into a trash bag.

That box was done. No, wait. One more thing at the bottom. Still bopping to the beat, Maryvonne reached down and picked up what looked like an ancient tin tube of toothpaste. The label read Testor, but she wasn't sure what this was. She was still dancing, and in a zealous moment squeezed too hard on the tube and it cracked and liquid began to puddle in her hand.

Just as Donna Summer's song was ending with an echoing *on the radio, radio, radio, radio…,* Maryvonne was overcome by the toxic fumes of whatever it was, staggered, and fell to her hands and knees on top of the old clothes where even more of the sticky goop squirted into her hand. In trying to catch herself, she succeeded in knocking over the remaining pile of magazines and doormats and sorted kitchen items with a loud crash.

Maryvonne was panting on her hands and knees in the pile when Zeus came out to check on the noise. Alarmed, he ran to her side and crouched down.

31

Immediately the fumes slapped him and he saw the broken Testor tube on one of the old doormats. Holding his breath, he scooped it up the sticky doormat and took it to the far side of the garage, and opened the garage door to bring in fresh air.

Maryvonne managed to twist around and sit down in the pile. She was wiping her hand with one of Zeus' old tee shirts, while blinking and taking deep breaths. "What was that?" she managed to gasp after a few more breaths.

"I'm so sorry. It's my fault; I should have warned you not to fool with that little tube. It's old model airplane glue from the seventies. They don't make that anymore because it is so toxic," Zeus replied, looking worried. "Are you hurt?"

"I don't think so. The tube disintegrated in my hand; I just got so dizzy I dropped myself onto the pile of clothes. I think I'm okay. Help me up and let's see."

Zeus pulled her up gently by the arms. She stood shakily, then began moving her arms and legs individually to see if there was any pain. "Bien. All seems in working order. Bof - those are some nasty fumes," she said as he took the stinking rags away from her and put them outside too.

"Go wash your hands right now," he instructed her. Get it off before it dries."

"Yes, and then I think I will go blow my nose and brush my teeth too. I have a weird taste in my mouth right up inside my head. I'll finish this sorting later."

"Good idea, I'll be right there. I just want to bag up all this toxic stuff right now, and save it for hazardous waste collection. I should have done that in the first place. Sorry," he said, chagrined.

Maryvonne turned to go, then went back to switch off the radio with her elbow. Just as she approached it the host came on. "Next up, *Boogie, Oogie, Oogie,* by Taste of

32

Honey." The word brought her mind back to poor Honey and she sighed.

In raising up her elbow to flick the switch off, she noticed something yellow stuck to the Velcro of her jacket cuff. She stared at the scrap of yellow cotton fabric. It was an old face mask she had sewn in the Covid days; it had a design of daisies, bees... and honey jars. The word was following her as she went in to wash up and take some ibuprofen.

She was feeling just a bit off in the head, so after she was all washed up, she decided to treat herself to a nice cup of hot chocolate. Not just any hot chocolate, but her special recipe she had dubbed "Goddess Hot Chocolate." The brew was highly healing and healthy.

She flipped the electric teapot on, and heaped a pile of Hershey's cocoa into a large mug. Then she added an equal amount of her thick, vanilla yogurt, which was loaded with probiotics, and a splash of water from the tap. She stirred it vigorously until it looked like brownie batter.

Then she drizzled a small dollop of fresh honey on the top; this made her think of poor missing Honey Lyman, and she sighed. This turn of events was truly heart-wrenching and bizarre. Maybe even sinister.

Into her mug, she added another small dollop of blackstrap molasses, topped it with a small scraping of coconut oil and stirred. The hot water was ready, but she waited five minutes for it to cool off some; she didn't want to kill off all the live goodies in the ingredients.

Picking up the teapot, filled the mug, and stirred the whole concoction until smooth. She took a nice long sip. The rich liquid chocolate flowed down her throat and made the world all right again.

~~~

33

Little Charlie arrived early the next morning. Maryvonne tried to take him two mornings a week to help out. He was her first grandson, so it must be said she tended to spoil him. He looked like a tiny but sturdy flaxen-haired Viking, and thankfully had a happy-go-lucky temperament.

"Za Za, I want to go see the train bridge, the turntable, and the train station."

"Yes, my darling cherub," she cooed as she pinched his chubby little cheek. "Let's watch Thomas first until it warms up outside, then later I'll pack some animal cookies and then we can go see the 10:15 train."

The speaking aloud of the time reminded her that it would be exactly twenty-four hours since Honey's casket to Hades exploded on the tracks. Still no word. Officer Bailey had taken her number and said she would text her when the body was located and the case was closed.

Soon, the hands on the clock showed it was time to go. "We're going to the train station," she said to Zeus, who was just putting the finishing touches on his soup.

"Of course you are! Can't keep my wife away from a mystery. We'll have soup for lunch when you two get back."

"Little Charlie loves it there; I can't keep him away from the train station just because it happens to be near the crime scene," she replied.

"Sure, whatever you say, dear. Behave."

"You can come with us, you know," she offered.

"Believe me, I would, but I have that Zoom meeting with the PUC at ten-thirty." Zeus volunteered for the town energy committee and was working on a project for municipal aggregation of electricity.

"Too bad!" she replied with a wicked smile.

"Behave!" he called one last time as Maryvonne and Charlie went into the garage.

34

Maryvonne loaded the tiny red balance bike and helmet into the trunk of her electric car, and found Charlie already sitting in his car seat waiting to get clipped in. Maryvonne stretched way over and clipped the buckle. Then she slipped his Cookie Monster sippy cup into the drink holder in his seat and closed the door firmly.

"Let's start today at the turntable, okay?" Maryvonne said, looking at him in the rear-view mirror. Little Charlie agreed, then blabbered on and on about what parts of the train he was going to look at today. He knew a lot about trains for a three-year-old. But then again, he did watch Thomas the Train every day.

Driving down Lincoln Street towards the train station, she passed by the cameraman driving a van out of the parking lot, going in the opposite direction. She wondered what he must have thought of the whole scene he had captured on video. It had truly been a ghastly freak show and would make a winning episode of some paranormal reality show like Ghost Hunter. Truth could be stranger than fiction at times. She shuddered as she relived the moment the casket blasted open, then tried to wipe that out of her mind.

Parking her car in the station lot, she unloaded Charlie and together they slipped through the gap in the chain-link fence and stepped onto the grass in the Heavenly Depot garden.

The sun was warm and the grass was just starting to green up from its brown winter coat. Charlie saw his first yellow dandelion of the season, exclaimed, and went over to pick it. "Look, Za Za! I'm going to put it in the drain," he said, crushing it deeply into his tiny pants pocket. He liked to drop flowers and acorns into street drains by the railroad bridge. Maryvonne nodded her head in acknowledgement.

Running over to the turntable, he stood holding the miniature rails at one end. Maryvonne took the opposite end in her hands and began walking slowly so that the turntable rotated. Charlie squealed in delight and said he was a diesel engine going to the shed for the night.

In the distance they heard the ringing bells of the first crossing gates going down, stopping traffic. Then the far-off whistle blast. The 10:15 would be on time today. Maryvonne looked over to see if the man in the grey shoes was on the platform today. He was not.

Little Charlie ran to the chain-link fence, gripping his tiny fingers into it and pushing his nose through an empty hole. The whistle blasted again, closer. "It's coming! It's coming, Za Za!" Charlie was jumping up and down.

Maryvonne stood behind him with her hands in her coat pocket, watching him and not the train. She couldn't get over the magic of his presence. The problems of the world seemed to fade when they were together.

The silver and blue Amtrak train came whooshing and clanking and hissing into the Exeter Train Station platform and the conductor put down the bridge and stepped out. A few passengers came out, then he called "All aboard!" and a few passengers got in. It was the same every time.

Little Charlie began chanting "All aboard, all aboard, all aboard..." causing Maryvonne to smile and tousle his hair. The conductor waved his arm and the engineer responded with a blast on the horn, which caused little Charlie to jump up and down again in his little black rubber boots.

As they watched the train move away, Maryvonne noticed a small figure standing in the window of one of the back rooms of the Curtain Factory, watching them.

It was Audrey Lyman. Maryvonne smiled and waved. Audrey smiled and waved back. She had often noticed Audrey looking out at the children as she sat at the sewing machine by the window. Taking little Charlie by the hand, she pulled him over to the window with some

36

difficulty. Audrey wrestled the old window open and stuck her blonde pixie-ish head out.

"Audrey, I am so sorry about your uncle. My condolences. Are you okay? Yesterday was just awful."

"Yes, much better today, Maryvonne. I nearly had a heart attack yesterday," she replied, the trace of a proper English accent shining through despite the sorrow.

"Me too, in a way. What a shocker. Glad to hear you are feeling better. Have the police found him yet?"

"Not yet," Audrey replied with a grimace.

"I had to go to the station yesterday so they could take my fingerprints because I had escorted Old Clive out back after the explosion. The police said that was a theatrical flash-pot or something. It sure looked real to me." Little Charlie was tugging on her arm and she shushed him.

"That bloody explosion sent me running right over here to the shop to catch my breath. What a terrible fright I had. Richard and my best friend Sylvia came with me, thank goodness. This building is my safe space and made me calmer. For some reason, it feels a woman's sanctuary inside these funny old walls."

Little Charlie had finally broken away and ran back over to play on the turntable again. Audrey smiled and said, "This is the best seat in the house for watching the little children play on that turntable."

"That's how I met you last year, when you were taking your lunch on the bench by Clive's Shasta daisies and I was spinning the turntable for my cherub. I was happy to meet the great-niece of my friend, Honey. Poor Honey; what in the world happened to him? I know he was a showman, but this feels very, very wrong. I hope for your sake it's over soon."

"Thank you, Maryvonne - I do too. He was a sweet old man, though I never really knew him well. Actually, I didn't really know him at all when I was

37

younger. He would visit us only once a year. Uncle Honey was so much older than my New York family, but I owe him a great debt for inviting me to come make my life in his town after my parents died," she began, then stopped and seemed to look far away for a moment before continuing.

"Uncle Honey drove down and got me when I was still traumatized, and helped me find a place to live here. He was the one that showed me the real estate ad for the Curtain Factory, and helped me figure out how to use my small inheritance to get a mortgage on it. The Hone-Lyman family line was always pretty small, and now that Uncle Honey has passed, it is just me." Audrey's big hazel eyes held a deep sadness as she said this.

Maryvonne's heart went out to the orphan. "I'm so sorry Audrey. Your uncle had a big heart, and at times he was larger than life. Honey will be missed by many."

Audrey sighed. Maryvonne stopped to wave to little Charlie who was running in circles around the turntable now. "Part of your family name was Hone? Is that why he was called Honey?" Maryvonne inquired.

"Yes, the Hone line is out of New York. One of our ancestors, Philip Hone, was a New York City Mayor during John Quincy Adams' term; he also wrote a juicy diary. Uncle Honey was the last to bear the Hone name in our line. It has died out with him."

"I always wondered about his name. It was a great stage name too," mused Maryvonne.

"I always thought it sounded so feminine and that any man would find it embarrassing, but he wore that cheeky name like a boss," she smiled.

"Yes, he sure did." Maryvonne pulled a card out of her purse and handed it to Audrey. "Audrey, please take my phone number. Give me a call sometime and let's go for a walk or have coffee or something. Or maybe have a glass of champagne in honor of Honey."

38

"I'd like that, Maryvonne. I think I should get out of this shop more often. I shouldn't even be here today, but I'm all at loose ends. Tomorrow is the weekend, and I've promised myself not to come in to work at all."

"Good idea. Spend time with Richard. Go for a hike or something and get some fresh air," Maryvonne said as she scooped up little Charlie, who had run back over to her. Audrey looked adoringly at the little boy, then said goodbye and closed the window.

"Za Za, I want to go on the train bridge now."

"Okay mon petit biscuit, let's jump back in the car and drive over to that bumpy old wooden bridge and get your bike out and glide around. After that we can go home for an early lunch, then mommy will be coming to get you.

"Train bridge, train bridge, train bridge…" he began chanting on the way to get into his car seat.

Maryvonne and her grandson had spent the entire morning together in constant motion. When mommy finally came to pick him up, Maryvonne went to take a quick nap.

Chapter 4

Bad Girls

When she awoke from her cat-nap, an idea had occurred to Maryvonne. Audrey had said the old Curtain Factory "felt like a woman's sanctuary inside those funny old walls." Perhaps Maryvonne could try to reach into that "women's sanctuary" with her mind… if she could get the "spangle" to work again.

The spangle had happened twice before, so maybe it could happen again. Twice before there had been mysteries, and twice before women from the past had reached out to her with clues which had enabled her to solve them. Okay, so this had been when she practically had a concussion and felt that her mind was altered temporarily because of it, but…

She had sniffed that glue yesterday, and had to admit she could still feel a slight headache bouncing around in there. Maybe the spangle would come, if she could get into the art-flow and coax it out. Just maybe.

And just maybe she could find Honey the mummy, and help Audrey with closure.

Was it dangerous? It felt so creepy down to her toes when she thought about Honey the mummy, but she was going to be brave and give it a try. The crazy scheme was not guaranteed to work, anyway.

She would not mention this to Zeus. No, no, no. One time before she had tried to explain the spangle, and he dismissed it out of hand and suggested she see a doctor to heal a concussion. Zeus was a man of science, but she was a woman of spirit.

Maryvonne knew that in order to get into the art-flow and coax out the visions of the past, she had to be deeply engaged in the creative process. In the flow. She had to be so engrossed in translating what she saw with her eyes in three-dimensions, into a two-dimensional rendering, that she could trick her conscious mind into letting other realities appear.

It was too cold to sit and paint outside today, her fingers would get too cold and distract from the flow, so she opted for a sketch.

Past Zeus' woodshop man-cave in a small room down in the cellar was her "art salon." She used it as her winter studio because the room had a large glass slider door to the backyard, so the light was good for a few hours in the afternoon. This is where she kept her art supplies alongside a large worktable. Over in a corner she found her old folding art stool and brushed the light layer of sawdust off with a rag.

Into her big art bag, she placed: a sketchpad, a small tin of Faber-Castell graphite pencils, and her trusty old kneaded gum eraser.

What else had she used in these plein-air circumstances? She hadn't been doing art outside since early last fall so nothing was prepared. Oh yes - her iPod with the purple earphones. The music this time would definitely be the disco. She had a killer disco play mix somewhere, and took a minute to find it and cue it up.

Zeus was just coming down the stairs to the man-cave to resume work on a Queen Anne highboy he had been constructing for nearly a year. As she passed through with her art gear, she stopped to admire his work. He was in the process of carving two seashell ornaments.

"You have mad skills, mon chéri, that is going to look lovely up in our dining room!" she enthused. "You've created a family heirloom. And look, the brass knobs and pulls you ordered have arrived." She picked up one of the shiny brass pulls, still in the shipping box, for a better look. "Oh, sorry, my dusty fingers are leaving prints all over the brass."

"Don't worry, when I finally put these beauties on, I will clean up both our prints and make sure they gleam like the sun," he replied, then looked at the art stool. "Ah, the first outdoor art session of the season? Good for

43

you. It will get your mind off the funeral. What are you doing?"

"A sketch of the old Curtain Factory."

He stopped putting the brass pulls back in the box and looked up at her. "Right next to the Heavenly Depot?"

"That's the place. It looks quite historically interesting," she said innocently.

"Behave yourself," he intoned.

"How much trouble can I get into just sitting and sketching?"

"Hrrmph."

"I adore you, mon chéri; the sunshine will do me good."

~ ~ ~

A chain link fence with a locked gate separated the far end of the Exeter Train Station parking lot from a professional moving company just past it. A fleet of large moving vans sat quietly behind the locked gate. Maryvonne pulled her electric car silently into the very last spot in the corner, quite near the moving vans.

From this secluded vantage spot, she could see the rear delivery door of the Heavenly Depot. This appeared to be an industrial style double-wide metal door. It stood flush to the asphalt in front of three crumbling parking spots, and was surrounded by a number of scruffy privacy bushes to shield the in-and-out of gurneys.

Had the mummy "escaped" by this exit? Or was the body still inside the funeral home, hiding? Or knowing Honey's hijinks, was there even a body? Old Clive had told her that he worked on the body all day, but could Old Clive be in on an elaborate scam? For what purpose? Follow the money, Zeus had said. Was there money?

She sighed, and looked around some more. From the angle on this side of the fan-shaped building that was the Heavenly Depot, she could also see a part of the front gardens. A young mother and her two children were playing on the slow-moving turntable. Audrey's workroom window was dark. The poor orphan girl seemed to have finally gone home.

Maryvonne opened the car door and got out. She opened the trunk and unloaded her stool and bag.

Voices floated over from the garden. "Callan, don't dig under there. That's not nice," Maryvonne heard the mom say to her young son, and she looked towards them at the tiny turntable. That turntable.

Old Clive was always puttering around that turntable. He had told her it was centered on top of the actual turntable that used to direct engines into the four-car house. Four sets of tracks had fanned out from it. One leading into each engine bay. That was why the Heavenly Depot building was fan shaped.

That meant that there must have once been a turntable mechanism underground, as well as four sets of track leading into, and out of, the engine house aka funeral home. Interesting foundations. Maryvonne's thoughts were interrupted by the ringing of the bells at the far crossing intersection.

The 1:27 was on its way to the Exeter Train Station. She had planned to set up her art stool near the platform just after the 1:27 left the station. She knew the station would be empty for a good while, since there was not another train due for hours, and it was nap time for all toddlers.

Over in the garden the little children were enthralled by the arrival of the train as they clung to the chain link fence.

It was the exact same every time. The silver and blue Amtrak train came whooshing and clanking and

45

hissing into the Exeter Train Station platform. The conductor would put down the bridge and step out. A few passengers would come out, then he would call out "All aboard!"

Maryvonne was halfway across the parking lot when she noticed the man with the grey shoes and black laces up on the platform. Aside from the funeral, she had not seen him since early fall, last year.

She narrowed her eyes and walked faster. She reached the base of the platform and pretended to look at the large schedule posted on a glass display case on the sidewalk. Her view was perfect.

Seconds before the train fully stopped, the man had placed himself at the far end of the platform, near the top of the stairs. This was the opposite end from where the conductor's door would stop. He then appeared to discreetly touch the train at hip level. Did he pull something off it and slip it in his pocket?

In the act of doing whatever he did, something tiny and purple went flying and landed a short distance from her. The man did not notice. "Hop-lá," Maryvonne whispered to herself.

She pretended to fumble in her bag while he came down the steps and got into his car.

Eyes scanning all over the car as it pulled away, she noticed it was a cream Lexus with tan seats. It had New Hampshire plates beginning with 283, and a parking sticker for Bubbling Brook retirement community.

After he left, she went back to pick up the tiny purple object. It appeared to be a pill. Score! She had some clues at last. Tucking the pill into a safe spot in her purse, she felt quite satisfied. And no harm done.

All the people had now dispersed and it was quiet. She turned her mind to the real task at hand. The sun was shining, and it was the warmest part of the day. Maryvonne

46

placed her art stool in the grass in front of the raised train platform, under a small fruit tree with swelled buds

The very long, faded grey section of the decrepit Curtain Factory rolled out in front of her, as she settled into a good position. Sketch book on knee, pencil tin open on the grass, she popped in her purple earbuds.

Now for the preamble; a moment to really look at the building with art-eyes. She studied the jumbled shapes: rectangles, squares, pointed gables, windows, doors. Then she looked at the shadows: bright noon sun on the roof, shading the portico entrance.

This was going to be a very geometric rendering. She preferred to insert some femininity into all her works. Where were the curves, the softness? Why was this building so long and plain? The best she could come up with to relay some type of femininity into the scene was to focus on the fancy swoops of the curtains of differing fabrics and styles in all the windows.

Hoping against hope that this would work, she was now grounded and ready. The iPod was poised in her hand; she took a deep breath and let it out slowly. "Allons," she whispered and hit play.

A second or two of delay… then a song by Donna Summer, that ultimate queen of the disco scene, came on. A single guitar scratched the funky rhythm, the horns folded in a few beats later, then a low and sharp police whistle, and the backup singers chanted...

> *Toot toot, hey, beep beep*
> *Toot toot, hey, beep beep*
> *Bad girls…*

Donna Summer's strong voice took over to tell the story of the bad girls while Maryvonne blocked in the jumble of shapes. Foreground: empty parking spaces ending in a wooden guardrail at the building. Midground: a

47

ditch after the guardrail. On the left, a long run of weathered clapboard with its many windows. On the right, the pell-mell roofline. In the center, the small bridge to the vestibule entrance and its faded canvas awning. Background: the far canopy of the trees.

The roofline hung her up for a while and she had to make liberal use of the gum eraser. The collection of additions on the side towards the Heavenly Depot proved to be a technical chore. As the struggle with the roofline was won, and she could feel herself slowly getting into the flow and the sketching became easier.

The music began to really grab her conscious mind, while the unconscious part relaxed into the flow and took over the art.

On the paper, the blocking-in was done, and the flavor of the scene was beginning to emerge. Now for the details. Sharp scratches of the hard pencil sang out as she constructed the window casings. Smooth swishes fell like summer rain as the soft pencil shaded under the long run of the eaves and the vestibule entrance. Her awareness of anything but the art and the music began to falter. The external world began to fade away.

More and more the disco music held sway over her ever-vigilant conscious mind. *Disco Inferno* came on and slowly carried her towards the abyss as her pencils scratched and swooshed the scene before her into life; clapboards, cornices, curtains.

Shake Your Groove Thing's driving beat hypnotized her monkey-mind, poised at the brink of awareness, as her pencils swooshed and scratched the scene before her into life: bridge, vestibule, lettering on the glass door.

Ladies' Night offered its invitation to join the party, and her mind was unknowingly coaxed over the edge as she rode along on the smooth rhythm, leaving the magic portal fully unguarded. Maryvonne felt the confines of her mind overhang, spangle, and switch to glide.

48

The door to the building was thrown open and a bevy of laughing women in long skirts with belted waists came tumbling out, their long hair piled in loose buns on the tops of their heads. Two appeared to be in their mid-thirties, the other maybe twenty years their senior.

The last of the younger girls stopped at the door, holding it open, as a man in jaunty knickers pushed a shiny bicycle out from inside and presented it to the older woman. "Congratulations on completing your cycling lessons, Mrs. Davis. Enjoy your new Rambler." He handed it to her with a smile, before disappearing inside.

"Mother, I knew you would love it," said the young blonde girl excitedly.

"I do love it, but my corset does *not* love it, I am going to have to invest in some of those looser corsets if I am to actually pedal this, Annie. You have some in the house, don't you? I'm going to have to take a closer look at the construction and see if I can't modify some of my older ones," said Mrs. Davis, trying to push her graying hair back under its loosened pins and push the bike at the same time.

Mrs. Davis looked to be a conservative middle-aged woman, dressed in a heather grey donegal tweed skirt and matching jacket. A high collared white shirt sporting a large, dark brooch at the throat, peeped out from under the tight-waisted jacket.

Annie encouraged her, "I am sure you can manage to adjust the corset, Mother, and become more unbound like us "new" girls. You have top-notch sewing skills; this new spring outfit you have fashioned me is lovely, and the slightly shorter skirt helps me move freely and stays out of the bicycle chain. I feel the height of fashion. Thank you."

Annie, a beaming girl wearing a dusky rose-colored skirt with a coordinating gingham-check blouse, took over the pushing of the bike for her mother, and the merry group stopped quite close to Maryvonne.

Maryvonne was thrilled that the spangle had come through so she could bear witness to this gift of the past. She knew from experience that she had to be still and soak up every word like a sponge.

The more heavy-set of the younger two women spoke up, chortling, "You know what, Kate? I have given up on those evil binders all together. I can't even bend over to look at a patient correctly. The male doctors don't have to put up with that foolishness, they're free to move about all they want. I won't compromise the health of my patients with that contraption anymore. I might just burn mine up, and you can throw yours on the pile too."

"Why Doctor Alice Chesley, who is going to come to see you when you won't even dress properly?" laughed the blonde fashion-plate Annie, elbowing her in the ribs. The pair seemed to be good chums.

"Plenty of women in this town, that's who," declared Dr. Alice.

The no-nonsense physician went on, "Women are so happy to not have a male poking around in their parts and dismissing their complaints, they wouldn't care if I was wearing bloomers. I have a mind to get myself a few pairs and get rid of this darned shroud of a skirt, which always seems to be in the way of my forward motion, dragging in the dirt until it is a rag, or hiding what I am looking for." She began batting at the cornflower blue broadcloth fabric of her full skirt in a disdainful way.

"You already scandalize the town by driving that automobile of yours, can you imagine if you wore bloomers as well? You may cause a riot," Kate Davis said with a sly smile.

"Humbug! Time marches on, Kate. It's a new world! Motor cars, electric trolleys, gas lights, telephones, and I just saw an ad for an electric wire to run from the power station right inside your house! The face of the world has changed right before our eyes in the last five years!"

Kate finished fixing her hair, and a few more people started coming towards the train platform, awaiting its imminent arrival.

Dr. Alice went on, "You know what has to be next, girls. Now that we are out of the bicycle shop, let's talk about the real issue; the women's vote." Discreetly, Dr. Alice stopped and looked around.

Satisfied they were not in earshot of the others, Dr. Alice went on in a subdued voice, "New Hampshire just has to vote yes on the state-wide referendum next week. 1903 is going to be the year of the woman, I can feel it in my bones. My part of the job is nearly complete: I'm picking up Mrs. Harriot Stanton-Blatch tomorrow here at the train station – in my motor car – and bringing her to her speaking engagement at the town hall. Then I'll drive her to Portsmouth shortly thereafter for her next engagement. How are you ladies doing on your end?"

Annie replied, "The announcement of Mrs. Stanton-Blatch's speech, and those letters to the editor requested by the New Hampshire Women's Suffrage Association have been sent into the Exeter Newsletter. I forwarded the one from Alice Stone Blackwell, and our own Walter E. Burt sent one in too. Tomorrow the entire town should see them in print! And of course, you saw Mr. Angelo Hall's letter in favor last week."

"Excellent job, Annie," nodded Dr. Alice in approval. "And you, Kate?"

"I've talked to all the women I can possibly think of in the Exeter Temperance Society and beyond. The vast majority is in agreement. They are going to do all they can to convince their husbands and fathers that women need the vote," replied Kate, wringing her hands.

Kate Davis shook her head and continued, "Alice, I am not as sure as you that we will win this vote. You

51

have to follow the money. If the woman's moral imperative is imposed by law upon all men, chances are some men could lose money. Money is the only thing that really convinces people, and most women don't own any, or own nearly anything else, according to current laws. That's exactly why I never remarried after I became a young widow so long ago. I want to be the captain of my own ship, and about the only way I can do it is to stay unmarried."

At that moment, a fancy motor car driven by a well-dressed middle-aged woman wearing a very fancy hat and gloves pulled into the station and parked. She jumped out lightly and flew towards them.

"Here's the exception to that rule, Mrs. Follansby, always supported by her husband in each and every action. He's a prince among men!" cried Dr. Alice.

Mrs. Follansby greeted the little group excitedly, then asked, "Is everything all set, ladies? My precious little Daisy is with her governess in the motor car, and Mr. Cutler should arrive at any moment, but I saw you gathered here and just had to run over and see you. We are here to greet a famous personage at the station and Daisy will present him with a small welcome bouquet. I regret I'm not allowed to speak his name quite yet, but you'll undoubtedly recognize him yourselves," she informed them hurriedly.

"Another illustrious guest for Mr. Cutler? That man is becoming the tip-top of Exeter-born men. Yes, Ella, everything is in motion. What about you, dear?" replied Kate, squinting towards the car to see the toddler.

"I've nearly worn out my welcome speaking to trustees, selectmen, physicians, and clergymen. I cannot be sure of my success. There were definitely some duds in there; Mrs. Dudley has taken it upon herself to rail against women's suffrage in similar circles. We have less than a week to persuade, and for the sake of the healthy family unit, I pray we succeed. There's so much work to do and so little time," replied Ella.

Then looking at the bicycle in Kate's hands, Ella chuckled and said, "It's a long way up High Street to our homes, Kate. Are you sure you have the strength?"

"Dear Lord, no. I am going to push it up that hill and never bring it down again. All I want it for is to ride it back and forth to the school house a few times, to show my pupils that you can teach an old schoolmarm some new tricks. My Annie is the one who will be riding it all over town, on her way back and forth to the Court Street school downtown. She is in line for a promotion, I am proud to report," replied Kate, in the fashion of proud mothers everywhere. Annie blushed, in the fashion of embarrassed progeny everywhere.

A low rumble approached, then a very fancy and shiny motor car pulled up beside Ella's. "I must run, here is Mr. Cutler. Good luck to us all!" she cheered. "Before I take my leave, let's seal our good luck with a Suffrage daisy-chain."

The women all hooked arms in a circle and said gaily in unison: "Daisies Forever." Then Ella broke off, towards her motor car and waiting child.

Maryvonne and the women all watched as the exquisite Mrs. Ella Follansby skipped merrily away: hat-feathers keeping time, the beautiful fabric of her heavy butter-colored silk outfit shining in the warm sun, full skirt flowing in the soft spring breeze.

Ella joined the man who stepped out of the passenger side of the fancy car, and together they made a striking pair, for he was no fashion slacker. His dark suit was crisply tailored, and his fingers flashed with diamonds reflecting the sun as he greeted Ella.

"Would you look at that; two of Exeter's highest flyers!" exclaimed Kate. "Old Rufus Cutler would be so proud of his son John G. today. My word! I wonder who they are greeting? Taking Mr. Follansby's advice and investing in a hotel at Hampton Beach was the best thing he ever did; now look at him. How many governors and US Presidents has he hosted at his swanky establishment? I've lost count." Kate smiled at the good fortune of John G. Cutler as he took off his hat and his tight black curls and ebony skin shone in the sun.

She continued, "I remember when he was a boy working in his father's dry goods store on Water Street. He inherited that and never looked back; I wasn't a big supporter of his Water Street billiard parlor, but it gave him the business experience he needed to make a top-shelf success of the Sea View Hotel over by Boar's Head. That man wears his many successful businesses around his neck like a string of pearls. Like I said, Old Rufus sure would be proud."

The governess had joined them with a tiny, golden-haired girl in a golden dress similar to her mother's, holding a small bouquet of posies in her tiny gloved hands. As this smart-looking group moved toward the train platform, others in the vicinity began to take notice of them as well.

Annie exclaimed, "Look how darling little Daisy looks today!"

Dr. Alice chimed in, "Yes, a little doll. And a lucky little girl, considering the entire sad affair between her parents, Georgette and Zephyr. I'm pleased we were able to preserve the little one's privacy, thanks to Mr. Follansby's contacts at the State House and Kate's brother, Officer Hamilton, who had to witness the sorrowful scene."

Annie replied, "Well if anyone deserves a beautiful child, it's Ella, and her husband certainly knows it. Good for them. Did you know that in her work with the State Board of Charities and Corrections she has placed nearly

54

two-hundred orphans? For a demure woman she is wonderfully ingenious and effective."

"My dear, she has placed more than that," Dr. Alice rejoined. "When I make my rounds at the colleges, there always tends to be a girl or two in trouble. Ella and I have a system where we place the mothers out of town until the child is born. If they want the baby, they keep it and start a new life, if not, then Ella works her magic. There is not a judge in the county or the next that she is not on a first-name basis with." A long steam whistle sounded from far off, interrupting her.

People were starting to crowd towards the train platform as the bell started ringing up at the far crossing on Front Street. Maryvonne could just see the crossing guard out in front of his tiny shack, ringing the bell by hand. She returned her gaze to the station. It was a bustling place. Many of the people gathered had now turned and were gawking at Mr. Cutler's motor car.

Dr. Alice lowered her voice to finish off her thoughts, "If I had been here when that handsome Greek boy Zephyr died in the mill accident and poor Georgette was so ill-served by the men doctors in town, Georgette would still be here to care for her baby girl."

Kate Davis added, "What a horrible tale that was. That little honey of a baby should be nestled in between Georgette and Zephyr right now. My word! But at least she has Ella. Let's go get that vote, girls, and help keep families better protected. Daisies Forever!"

Kate Davis' voice was drowned out by the train which came whooshing and clanking and hissing into the Exeter Train Station. The conductor put down a small block of steps. A few passengers came out, then he called "All aboard!" and a few passengers got in. It was the same every time… and had been for a long, long time.

Then, a vibrating spangle inside her skull and - wham-bam-thank-you-ma'am - Maryvonne was back from

55

Suffragette City. She became aware she was sitting on her art stool, decidedly alone. Her disco playlist had cycled all the way through and was repeating again. Before she pulled the purple earbuds out of her ears, she became aware of a chunk of the lyrics from *Bad Girls*...

> *Now you and me, we're both the same*
> *But you call yourself by different names*

Chapter 5

I Will Survive

Maryvonne blinked a few times, and closed her mouth which had been gaping since the mention of Georgette and Zephyr. She knew that story.

Everyone in town knew that old ghost story, and it came back to life regularly, especially at Halloween. It filled every woman with dread at the thoughts of the lack of choices for pregnant women and girls back then.

The lore went like this. Georgette was a pretty French immigrant who worked at the Exeter cotton mill on the river. Exeter's cotton mill had woven Southern bales of cotton into fabric bolts since the early 1800's. It had grown to be a very large and profitable enterprise. By the 1850's, the business had been expanding and new immigrants were hired in large numbers, but not local, literate, Blacks.

The orphan Georgette was a quiet girl who worked long hours in the mill and lived in the mill dorms. She didn't speak English very well, but she was kind and well-liked by the other girls.

Although Georgette tried to keep to herself, due to her wholesome beauty she had caught the eyes of a few rogue male managers at the mill. These foul men had made an unholy competition amongst themselves as to who could molest her in the vilest manner. They groped her and pressed themselves up against her when no one was looking. Often there was more than one of them cornering Georgette in the bobbin room, or any small nook they could find. They even followed her home at times, though appearing not to.

They were discreet, and the upper managers and mill owners had little idea of their wretched behavior. Poor Georgette was bruised, battered and ashamed, but had no means of recourse because she was an orphan who barely spoke the language. But she needed that job, she had no options. So, she just kept silent.

Enter Zephyr. Recently arrived from Greece via France, this handsome young man was poly-lingual and became aware of poor Georgette's distress. In time, he confronted the gang. Unfortunately, one of the cads was his superior and threatened to fire him.

To counter this, Zephyr swore to Georgette that he would escort her as much as possible to thwart the gang's clandestine attempts. He would walk her to and from work, and never be too far away from her bobbins. Poor Georgette was very grateful, and took him as her confidante. Soon they became secretly engaged to be married.

Zephyr's diversions worked for a while, but before long the gang figured out what he was up to and the decided to ambush Zephyr.

The resulting brawl ended with Zephyr's body mangled in a horrific "mill accident." He bled out quickly and died on the spot. Poor Georgette was beside herself, and the wicked gang was immediately fired by the mill owners, but skipped town before they could be charged for a crime.

Georgette continued working for months, pale and silent at her bobbins, all the while trying to hide that her waist was growing thicker. Finally, she was found out by the mill owner and called from the factory floor to the head office.

Old Doc Lawton, who disliked having to treat the mill girls, was called in to confirm her case, and he found her to be well along. The mill owners would not have her bad example lead others astray and they dismissed her from job and house. Doc Lawton said that when the baby came in a month or two, he would take it away from her, as she had no prospects.

Georgette, an orphan herself, dearly wanted the baby. The child was her only family. Desperate times called for desperate measures, and she disappeared before the next day's sun had set.

About a month later, two young boys were stalking squirrels with slingshots in the misty cemetery. The sun was dipping behind the trees and the shadows grew long across the headstones. One boy stooped to pick up a fresh stone, and felt it was wet. Curiously, he turned it over in his hand and found it to be clotted with sticky red blood. Under his feet in the dimming daylight, he was startled to see a trail of blood. He called to the other boy in fright.

The two boys looked in horror to see a trail of blood leading from Zephyr's grave to the door of the half-constructed brick receiving morgue. The small, ornate combination morgue and chapel was only an outer shell, the construction having been delayed over a year now.

Approaching the closer of the two doors, they saw great puddles of blood creeping out from under it, almost running down the path of the cemetery. Screaming and pushing, they both streaked home as fast as they could.

The police came quickly, though now it was pitch dark. Their lanterns shone in the puddling blood at the door. One officer and the two boys' fathers all stood aghast in the jagged shadows as the policeman prepared to open the door.

As the officer put his hand to the knob, they suddenly heard a sharp, high-pitched cry from inside, which sent one of the fathers bounding away in terror.

The police officer steeled his nerves, and burst open the door to the grisly scene.

In the center of a makeshift, blood-soaked bed piled with covers was the pale, dead, form of Georgette. Beside her the ripped placenta lounged in a pool of blood. She had strapped the baby to her breast with a large shawl, and the pitiful baby was alive and suckling the cold breast in between screams.

Old Doc Lawton was called for quickly. He tsked, pronounced Georgette near twenty-four hours dead, and scooped up the infant to warm and clean it. He found the placenta was still attached, and clamped it off and cut it with tools from his bag. The cold, hungry infant screamed bloody murder at the doctor's touch.

Newspaper accounts said it was apparent that Georgette had hid out in the receiving chapel area of the half-completed building for a month's time in an attempt, against all forces, to keep her baby. The town was abuzz. Some people had seen her pilfering vegetables from their gardens, but looked the other way. Some people had seen smoke coming out of the chimney at night, but looked the other way.

Poor Georgette apparently had an early and hard labor all alone, then dragged herself over to Zephyr's grave to show him the baby before returning to expire from blood loss, as her beloved Zephyr had done before her.

As for the much-wanted baby, Georgette had shown incredible forethought by strapping the baby to her breast. This enabled the baby to survive, even as she faded away.

The story was so tragic that certain townsfolk, those that had looked the other way, paid for a proper burial for Georgette. She was buried beside her lover, Zephyr, for eternity.

But the tragic tale did not end there, it grew and grew and was embellished upon until it became a town legend.

Every once a while, even up to present day, someone walking in the cemetery would claim to have seen orbs or other ethereal shapes of either or both of the lovers walking, always barefoot, towards or away from the brick receiving morgue. Their footprints always tracked the blood up and down the walkways.

Maryvonne had heard this "river of blood" story many times, and it always ended with the doctor sending the infant to the orphanage as originally planned by old Doc Lawton.

However, what she had just witnessed told her that Ella Follansby and her circle of strong women had rapidly intervened and changed the luck of that baby.

It seemed that the babe born in the cemetery was now enjoying a splendid, white-gloved life.

Finally, the shock of the Georgette story began to abate. Maryvonne turned her thoughts to the many other things she had just learned from the group of women. It had been like watching an episode of The Golden Girls on television; so much chatter all at once.

Maryvonne did know that women finally won the struggle for the vote in 1920. What she didn't know was that the issue of Women's Suffrage was on the town ballot in Exeter in 1903! And she had never heard that a famous American Suffragette, Mrs. Harriot Stanton-Blatch, had spoken in the Exeter Town Hall in favor of it. Maryvonne knew Stanton-Blatch to be the daughter of Elizabeth Cady-Stanton of Seneca Falls, New York - the woman who had first put her pen to paper and scribed the "Declaration of Sentiments."

That brought history off the dusty page and into living color. It wasn't just famous women in New York that were working hard for the vote, it was average women in Exeter too.

She'd never heard of any of the four local women who appeared to be fighting for the vote on behalf of women and families. It tickled her that some of them lived on High Street, which was her street. Where, exactly?

She'd never heard of John G. Cutler. Shouldn't she have? All the other rich guys of yesteryear had their names plastered all over the town and the history books. Why was his success story wiped from the town history?

He seemed a serial entrepreneur. She wondered if any of his buildings still existed.

After letting all this soak in for a moment, she packed up her art supplies, her stool, and returned to her car in the far corner. Relaxing against the comfortable, supportive seatback, she sat there for another ten minutes while she wrestled with what part of the interaction had held to clues to Honey's whereabouts.

Kate had said to follow the money. Annie said she was unbound by old corsets, Alice had said things were hidden by her skirts, and what did the whole story about the baby Daisy have to tell her? Or the bicycles?

All this talk would need to sit in the crock pot of her mind until it gelled into something useful. From experience, Maryvonne knew it would come at some point.

She also needed to spend some time on her laptop and research some of these names and stories. That might help clarify the terms of the puzzle.

And then there was the little purple pill from the man with the grey shoes. She had to work on that too. At once, she felt overwhelmed and just plain tired-out from the past two days. It was time to go home and just let it all go for the rest of the day. Maybe she would make herself a nice mug of hot-chocolate, goddess-style.

~ ~ ~

Spending the past two nights with Sylvia's family had done a world of good for Audrey. It had been a dreadfully long time since she felt the warmth of a family circle around her. Mark was a great therapist and had been thoughtful in his discussions with her after dinner for two evenings.

He helped her to see that perhaps she had declined Richard's marriage proposal and pushed him away out of fear of the past repeating itself. Audrey could see

63

now that to be married with children of her own, and to help all children, was her heart's true desire.

Audrey had decided that she would commit to seeing a therapist regularly for the next six months before making any moves. Mark offered to give her a list of names to choose from. Since her parents had died, she realized she had been a ticking time bomb, putting her life on hold, waiting for the explosion. Neither she nor Richard deserved that.

Today she was on her way to the lawyer's office. Attorney Debra Bacon had been leaving messages for two days on her cell phone about Honey's will, but Audrey couldn't bring herself to return the call until this morning. She had finally called back Richard as well. When he found out about the lawyer's appointment, he offered to join her so she wouldn't have to go alone.

Richard picked her up in his SUV, and drove her to the nearby city of Portsmouth for the appointment. He seemed very nervous while he was driving, almost crashing into another car in the parking lot. Audrey's nerves were on edge too.

Audrey saw etched on the fancy glass door that this was a branch of a Manhattan legal firm. Furrowing her brow, she began to wonder about Honey. He was a man of mystery to be sure, he had held his cards close to his pocket the entire time she had known him. And now he had disappeared to boot. It was just dreadful.

Audrey did not want to be here, but Ms. Bacon had seemed adamant.

Richard held the door open and they passed into a rich interior: darks walls, leather furniture, large artworks on the walls. Richard announced their names to the receptionist and they took a seat in the waiting room.

After a few minutes, the receptionist returned and escorted them into a large, well-appointed conference room with a large mural of early American scenes covering one entire wall. Another assistant entered and politely inquired if they would enjoy some hot tea. Audrey gratefully accepted. Richard nervously declined.

The assistant left the room to fetch the tea, and Ms. Bacon entered and introduced herself with a firm handshake and a twinkling of her blue eyes. She expressed her condolences as the assistant returned silently and placed the steaming tea in front of Audrey.

Ms. Bacon went on to say that under the unusual circumstances, the execution of the will would be delayed until further notice. Audrey nodded and blew on her tea before taking the first sip. Ms. Bacon paused a moment to ask if the tea was okay. She then relayed that also under the unusual circumstances, a police detective had requested to join in the official reading of the will. At that moment the door opened and a plain-clothes detective joined them.

Audrey's eyebrows shot up in surprise as he offered his condolences and sat down in a chair well off to the side of the conference table. Under the table, Richard wrung his hands and stared at Audrey.

The moment had come. Ms. Bacon commenced with the reading of the documents in front of her, starting with the preamble of "I, Albere Hone Lyman, being of sound mind…" and going on to state that he was leaving his entire estate to his only surviving relative, Miss Audrey Lyman.

Ms. Bacon continued reading: "…to include my entire stock portfolio, which I inherited from my father before me, Robert Albere Hone-Lyman, and he from his father before him, Philip Hone, estimated at seven million dollars." Audrey lurched forward at this news and spilled her tea on the table. Ms. Bacon called for the assistant. Richard blanched and grasped the arms of his chair. The detective observed this all, with no show of emotion.

~~~

Backstage at the prep school theater, Jefferson Reed hid behind a rack of costumes and popped another antacid in his mouth. He could kill Honey.

He could hear the students on the stage, helping each other run through their lines. Jeff was trying to hold it together, but just didn't seem to have the bandwith to focus on his job while he was a "person of interest" in a crime.

Honey's final parting scene, which he had agreed to supervise all those years ago, had gone way off the rails. Literally. When the casket came up the rails and stopped beside him, he had detonated the flash-pot, as he had been instructed by Honey himself. Then he was to run off the stage in fright, and go into the back room. That part had gone perfectly to script.

The next instruction was to wheel the mummy onto the stage and request applause for Honey's final theatrical caper. But when he got in the back room, Honey the mummy was not on the gurney in the private family room where he had left him moments before, his small body all wrapped up and stiff as a board. Jefferson was shocked. He ran through all the back rooms looking for him, even pulling out all the morgue drawers.

When he heard Old Clive and Maryvonne coming into the back rooms, he panicked and slipped through the rear delivery door, cut through the scruffy bushes, and highballed it back to his apartment in shock. As his long legs carried him briskly home, he prayed to God that Honey's body would show up. How could it not?

But it indeed did not.

The police came looking for him within an hour and asked him to come to the station to take his deposition and prints. Jeff spilled his guts at the station.

The police were not sure what to make of his story and held him for an hour while the Heavenly Depot

66

fingerprints were being collected. His prints were indeed all over everything, the brass pulls of the casket, the doors of every back room, and the heavy pulls of every single morgue drawer.

Jeff's wife was called during that same hour, and Jeff had directed her where to locate a certain folder. She found it and brought it to the station. In the folder, in Honey's hand, was the "funeral script" and stage directions for his final scene on this earth.

That evidence satisfied the police for now, but they told Jeff not to leave town. And they also forbade him to speak of it to anyone, while the investigation was ongoing.

The police did mention there was one remaining set of unidentified set of prints. Jeff took that as a veiled threat that they were looking into his accomplice. But he did not have an accomplice, and was pretty sure he was the very last person out back before the Casket Caboose started clicking along. He felt anxious that he was to be railroaded into a false confession.

It had been two full days now, and the mummy was still on the loose. Jeff wasn't sure how much longer he could survive the strain.

"Mr. Reed? Mr. Reed? Where are you?" a young actor was calling backstage. Jeff slipped the roll of antacids back in his jeans pocket and dug his way through the costume rack full of outfits for the upcoming play, *The Secret Garden*.

Jefferson Reed was going to have to survive at least until the end of the school day. He sighed, then filled his lungs and shouted, "Here I am Piper, what can I help you with?"

~~~

Meanwhile the hashtag #ExeterMummySightings was trending across the NH Seacoast social media.

According to eyewitness reports the mummy had been seen: ordering an egg and ham croissant at the Dunkin Donuts drive-thru in Kingston, crashing the gates at the Hampton toll booth, stealing bandages from the Seabrook Urgent Care walk-in center, paddle-boarding in the Atlantic Ocean near the Cinnamon Rainbows Surf Shop, and riding the purple dinosaur at the local playground.

Officer Bailey Barndollar looked at her smart phone incredulously and hoped to God that she would not be sent out to any of these dubious places to ask questions.

Chapter 6

Shame

By Saturday morning, between pondering the clues from the "Golden Girls" - Kate, Annie, Alice and Ella - and the ridiculousness of the social media posts, Maryvonne thought she would lose her mind. The words to Evelyn "Champagne" King's disco hit *Shame* were playing in a loop in her head.

> *You got me so confused*
> *It's a shame*
> *Sometimes I think I'm going insane*
> *But still I want to stay*

Maryvonne did wonder if she was going insane after seeing the social media chatter. She needed a reality check and needed it fast if she was to keep her sanity. She decided to make a phone call to get the facts.

The crack historian at the Exeter Historical Society was a friend of hers, and she would be able to help Maryvonne sort the wheat from the chaff. This bespectacled woman was full to the brim with knowledge of both town facts, and town lore, also known as "fake news." The townsfolk had affectionately nicknamed her "Brim."

Maryvonne had done some preliminary research on her laptop, so that she only needed to ask the Brim a few questions to fill in the gaps. That would give Maryvonne better context to stitch the puzzle together.

Soon, she was connected and exchanging greetings on the phone. After a quick personal catch-up, Maryvonne said she was interested in hearing about Exeter's Suffragettes.

Brim replied, "First off, Suffragettes was coined in the English press as a term that made fun of the female Suffragists. The term is used somewhat interchangeably today, but scholars always say Suffragist, which could mean a man or a woman. Then sometimes it was shortened even further to 'Suffs' when reporters were trying to save space in printed materials."

"I see," replied Maryvonne and thought for a moment "But you know, I like the word Suffragette anyway. It seems livelier; Suffragist seems stuffy. Suffs is even more fun; it sounds like a team name. Anyway, I'm especially interested in these names: Kate and Annie Davis, Dr. Alice Chesley, and Mrs. Ella Follansby," she began and paused to give the Brim a chance to jot down some notes.

Maryvonne started again, "I've seen a decent amount of information online regarding Dr. Chesley, as she was one of Exeter's first female doctors and lived a very long life. But I can't find anything on the others at all."

Brim kicked right into brim-mode. "Well, Mrs. Kate H. Davis was a long-time leader of the Exeter Women's Christian Temperance Union and wrote tons of letters to the editor on many topics. She was born here, her maiden name was Hamilton, and she married into the Davis family as a young girl. She was made a widow when she was only twenty-two, and never remarried. Already, she had an infant and a toddler. She taught for twenty years or so at a school on Prospect Hill. It was actually on the corner of Auburn and Magnolia," Brim said precisely.

Brim took a breath and went on, "Now, Annie Davis was one of her daughters, and she never married. She was also a teacher, and actually became the principal at the Court Street school, now known as the Parks and Rec Building." Brim paused.

Maryvonne interjected, "So these two were active in Exeter in obtaining the women's vote?"

"Yes, Kate was the driving force. And believe it or not, there was an Anti-Suffrage party in town," she chuckled. "That was led by a Mrs. Francis Dudley, daughter of the long-time town physician. So, the Exeter 'fors' and 'againsts' went at it non-stop for a while, until

1920 when the Nineteenth Amendment was finally ratified. Then they all got together to help with registration and education on issues."

"I see. But what about the 1903 town vote on the New Hampshire State-wide referendum?" inquired Maryvonne. She couldn't find much online information on that date in regards to Exeter.

"That did happen, but we have little information on it ourselves. It seems pretty under-documented. The outcome was about tied…. maybe 105 yes and 110 no. So, the Exeter men voted it down, but slimly. They were afraid of what they called 'petticoat rule' and that women would take away their booze."

Maryvonne spoke, "Mon Dieu, what a long seventy-year battle to get that done! And everyone still has their booze, too. Next: I know about Dr. Alice, but couldn't find a thing on Mrs. Ella Follansby."

"The name sounds familiar, let me look in my files and see. I'll get back to you. I think she must have been the wife of William Follansby. I can tell you about him first. He was a wealthy man with a string of dry goods stores around the State. He moved to Exeter and became a bank president, then a State Legislator – say around 1895. He was powerful – on the Governor's Council and I think maybe he was a commissioner on several electric utility and railway outfits. This was when electricity was first taking the country by storm, so it was a really big deal. It was like vertical marketing and people were making tons of investments and profits. Electric trolley tracks were being laid everywhere. Possibly Follansby was also a commissioner on the task force assembled to develop Hampton Beach as a tourist destination for the masses by running the trolleys there and beefing up the amenities. The Casino Ballroom you still see today was part of that project. But that was him; let me see what I can dig up on her. You know, back then it would be an embarrassment for a wife of a man like that to have her name in print anywhere."

Brim stopped and made a boo-hiss noise. "That is how people felt back then, but you know what the bumper sticker says: 'Well-behaved women seldom make history.' It's kind of a shame, because then we don't have clear paper trails of the contributions that women were making back then. They get erased from history. Get it: HIS-story?" she guffawed.

Maryvonne giggled, "You astound me with all the HIS-tory you carry in your head."

Brim then became more serious, "The things society can learn from history, such as how *not* to repeat mistakes, are very important, and that's one reason why I feel called to be a historian."

Maryvonne agreed, then remembered something else. "Hey - so you mentioned Hampton Beach. I am also wondering about John Garrison Cutler, the hotelier. I see info online on him, but it mostly talks about his time in Hampton Beach at the Sea View Hotel, giving lists of sitting US presidents and legislators who spent time there in the summers. John G. actually named one of his sons Charles Sumner after the famous anti-slavery senator from Massachusetts who often stayed there. John G. had so many State and Washington politicians stay at his place that older historians painted him as a 'Kingmaker' of the Republican party, and called his hotel a Summer White House. Do you know anything about his early life in Exeter?" inquired Maryvonne.

"Yes indeedy. John G. Cutler - born around 1833 or so if I remember correctly - was the grandson of Tobias Cutler, a Revolutionary War veteran, and Dorothy Paul, one of Caesar Paul's mulatto daughters. Yuck, I don't like that word 'mulatto' it means little mule or something. I think I am making an executive decision right now that I'm never going to use that old word again. It seems

73

dehumanizing," Brim stopped for a minute, as if sealing that decision into her mind.

Brim cleared her throat, then went on, "Sorry, I digress. Now, Caesar Paul was brought here from Africa at the age of fourteen and became enslaved to a man in Exeter as a house-servant. He would have been one of John G.'s great-grandfathers. His grandfather, Tobias Cutler, earned his freedom from enslavement by fighting in the Revolutionary War, so his son, Rufus, was born a free man. Rufus, John G's dad, opened a very successful dry goods store on Water Street, and the whole family lived upstairs. After he died John G. ran the store and lived upstairs with his mom. Later, John G. also owned and operated a billiards parlor in the basement of the store next door. He was a businessman to the core, and did not marry until he was fifty. He married a white woman named Harriet Brewster around the time the building burned in 1873."

Maryvonne interjected, "You remember the exact date when his shop burned? That's astounding!"

"Well, it wasn't just his shop. That fire is known as the Great Conflagration and three full blocks of Water Street shops burned one night. The fire started in the chimney of one of the upstairs rooms after he and his mother had gone to sleep. And it spread up and down the block, burning out eight buildings full of businesses."

"Mon Dieu! What a shame!" exclaimed Maryvonne.

"Yes, it was memorable. Cutler's building and the two that flanked it were in his family for forty years. His father, Rufus, built it. His in-law, George Harris, built and ran a shop next door, where the bookstore is now. After the fire, John G. used his insurance money to rebuild the middle building, but the ones on the sides got incorporated into the new, large brick buildings you see today like the Carlisle Block and Phillips Wharf. A bit more fireproof.

Shipments of goods came directly to the wharf from ships that would sail up the river; the river was much deeper then. John G's historic building still stands today at 127 Water Street, and is now owned by Martin Family Enterprises."

Really?" exclaimed Maryvonne, surprised. "Does it have a plaque on it or something? I can't remember seeing anything like that around. I'm going to check it out today when I go over to the bookstore for the LitFest events later this morning."

"No plaque as far as I know. But to continue the story: John G. then also buys, for whatever reason, a small place at the beach called the Sea View Cottages. It was in the north part of the oceanfront strip, up by the entrance to the Boar's Head. It was near where the wealthy and powerful - like the Follansbys and folks before them like Franklin Pierce - had their summer mansions. The whole of the beach was actually a playground for the wealthy back then, as it was off the beaten track. At some point, not sure when, John G.'s mom moves in with his brother Nathanial, who had a barbershop business downstairs -and his home upstairs - on Portsmouth Ave, where the Walgreens is now. Around that same time, John G. gets married to Harriet and moves to the beach full-time. His hotel becomes one of the only ones open year-round, catering to the wealthy. And later on, trolley tracks are laid from the Exeter Depot practically to his back door at the beach. So, he rode that wave."

Maryvonne was taking it all in, but something was missing. "Sea View Cottages? I thought it was a big hotel?"

"Yes, cottages at first," the historian replied. "But like many wooden buildings of that era, it too succumbed to fire. About ten years after he bought it, it burned just before the beginning of the summer season. But Cutler had it rebuilt in a capacious and elegant manner in only thirty days; I guess it helps to have friends in high places.

Ten-term US Representative for New Hampshire, Cy Sulloway, summered there for many years, holding forth on the large front porch. Lots of writers stayed there too like Holmes, Whittier and Thaxter. Even Tom Thumb and PT Barnum stayed, as well as General Robert E. Lee. Imagine that! Cutler couldn't let his important guests down because of a fire, so the new 'Cutler's Sea View House' opened in time for the Fourth of July. Cutler went on to add a very large restaurant next door with a dozen or so more rooms upstairs, a billiard hall just behind that, and a stable for forty horses. Just query 'Cutler's Sea View, Hampton' or 'Hotel Era Hampton Beach 1800's' online and you can read more about it," she finished.

"Thanks. I'll do that. Is it still there? Maybe I'll drive by it next time I go to the beach," Maryvonne said.

"It was there for one hundred years. Burned in 1985, I think. The only thing still standing is the restaurant, which is now called 'Ron's Landing,' and a small road runs around to the back of the old complex still named 'Cutler Ave.'"

"I've been to Ron's Landing many times! I had no idea of its origins," exclaimed Maryvonne. "Did their children take it over after they died?"

"No. John G. had it forever. Towards the end of his life, he also did some other development there too. He bought an undeveloped area on the approach to the beach and put in a road and sectioned it off into plots. It is still called Glade Path. Look on a map. He died at about eighty years old, around 1913; just when Hampton Beach had lost its name as a playground for the rich and famous, and the thronging masses were taking over. He and Hattie did have two sons, but one died as a child and the other as very young man. Sad."

"Yes, that is very sad," replied Maryvonne. "So, John G. was quite the successful business man, but maybe very sad in private with his wife. Oh, I can't imagine the loss for Hattie too. Both children! Horrible! What happened to the hotel after they died?"

"I don't know. He died first, and I think Hattie sold it and moved to Miami or something. But, to end the story, John G. and his family have a large gravestone over in Hampton. But his parents are in the Exeter cemetery with a sturdy, square pink granite marker. And his grandparents are in the old Winter Street Burying ground, over by the famous patriot Jude Hall. The two Black patriots have stones next to each other. I like to think that when Abraham Lincoln gave his anti-slavery speech at the Exeter Town Hall in 1860, that Rufus and his sons were in attendance in honor of their patriotic ancestor."

"I guess we'll never know, unless a diary turns up or something. Now, I find it interesting that John G. made a good start in Exeter, but then went out of town to make his real fortune," mused Maryvonne. "It's a shame, he's not more well-known in Exeter."

"Anything else I can help you with today?" asked the Brim.

"No. But merci beaucoup. You have given me so much of your time today already. I appreciate it," declared Maryvonne. "But wait, there is one more thing. Is there an easy way to find out the old addresses of all these people we talked about without taking up any more of your time?"

"Yes, just go over to the public library and look at the old phone books in their archives room."

"That's easy, thanks," replied Maryvonne.

The two then said their goodbyes as Zeus shuffled into the room holding his shoes. He sat down and started to put them on while saying, "I'm almost ready to go the LitFest downtown and check out the event. What about you?"

"Just give me five minutes and I'll be ready too." Later in the day she was going to have to process all the info Brim had just given her. Her head was already swimming, and the day had just begun.

Chapter 7

Never Can Say Goodbye

The day was turning out to be another warm one, so they decided to take the Zeus-mobile.

"Let's put the top down," suggested Zeus.

"Are you kidding? It is not nearly warm enough for me," replied Maryvonne. "Plus, it will give me bad hair and people will wonder if I'm a witch. You know, the schedule this year is heavy on spooky authors."

"Then you'll fit right in. The top is going down; it's only a mile. I'll drive slowly for your hair. But the car is just begging me to put down the top today, and I must obey its command."

Maryvonne got in and pulled her hair into a ponytail as he put down the top. She had to admit, there was nothing quite like driving on a sunny day with the top down. Even though it was a trifling thing in the grand scheme of life, it gave her such pleasure.

As they pulled up, Ellen Swartz was outside the indie bookstore downtown on Water Street taping the day's schedule to a large sandwich board. Maryvonne jumped out of the car and ran over to give her friend a big hug.

Ellen exclaimed, "I see you have the top down already. Beach season is practically just around the corner, and I can't wait!"

She and Maryvonne had a standing date on Thursdays in the summer at Hampton Beach. They would jump in the convertible and enjoy the fifteen-minute drive to the coast. Ellen brought the tuna sandwiches, and Maryvonne brought the chips. They would then commence doing nothing at all on their beach blankets and chairs, for four to five hours, and doing it consummately. They were beach bums, and delighted in it.

"I can't wait either, I miss the salty air," sighed Maryvonne.

"And I miss the fish nibbling our feet," joked Ellen.

"Yuck, I hate that! Nasty giant sea bass, they send me screaming out of the water every time!" tittered Maryvonne.

Ellen, a tall woman with a killer sense of humor and an infectious laugh, chortled too. She tucked some of her curly brown hair behind her ears, and then her heavily-lidded brown eyes looked behind Maryvonne. "And here comes your better half; hello, handsome!" she greeted him.

Zeus joined them on the sidewalk. "Hello, Ellen, nice to see you. Looks like another great schedule this year, nice job. I love a good ghost story, and it looks like you have a couple of interesting paranormal authors."

"Oh yes! – we're fortunate to have so many authors in this little town, and books about this town. It's virtually an embarrassment of riches, so it makes it kind of easy. The owners of the bookstore, Stan and Effie, select the authors every year; they know everyone, far and wide. Then my team does the logistics, PR, and coordinates the volunteers. Did you hear that our group just became a non-profit, so we can apply for grants and make sure the festival stays free to the public?"

"Congratulations!" replied Zeus, "I saw that announcement in the papers. I know a lot of year-round work goes into producing the weekend festival."

"It does get pretty consuming in the last month," replied Ellen, "but by tomorrow we'll all get to rest for a while before we start over. Look, I'd love to kibbitz more but I've got a ton of little things to attend to this morning, sorry."

"Of course," Zeus and Maryvonne replied in unison.

"Enjoy the festival," Ellen called after her as she picked up her clipboard and headed towards the town hall, another of the venues.

The LitFest was held in many downtown buildings, the large and historic old town hall being one of them. The main floor held seating for three hundred and a large stage. On the upper level it had a large, well-lit art gallery, and a filming studio.

Zeus and Maryvonne stood looking at the schedule on the sandwich board together. A day ago, they had decided that they would attend the paranormal author's talk together in the morning in the bookstore. Then they would browse the art show in the town hall, and split up after that.

Zeus would go see author Norm Phillips talk about his book detailing his time as a WW2 fighter pilot and then walk home. Maryvonne would stay in the gallery and see author Lara Morter, the private investigator turned mystery writer. Maryvonne would finish the morning at a spiritual writer's event in the Salt Cave, then drive the car home for lunch.

People were filing past them into the indie bookstore where "Karloff's Paranormal Tales of Exeter" would begin in just a few minutes. Zeus pulled Maryvonne by the hand and they entered the crowded room to look for a pair of open seats. As they settled in, Maryvonne said to Zeus, "I hope this isn't too scary."

To which Zeus replied, "I hope they talk about that old Nathaniel Gilman admin house on Front Street. I've heard about that one many times over the years. A few of my colleagues won't even work in there alone. I think hauntings are bunk, but I love to hear the preposterous tales that are made up." Maryvonne held up two fingers in the sign of the cross, grimaced and shrank in her seat.

At the head of the room, the podium was draped in a black cloth, and in front of it was a small table, also draped in the cloth. Official ghost hunting instruments were labelled and displayed on the table; a thermal camera, an electric blue probe, various meters and recording devices.

Maryvonne eyed them thoughtfully and wondered if any of those technological wonders would get a reading on, or recording of, things she saw during her spangle-times. Maryvonne had been unsuccessful in deciphering any clue out of her research so far. It was dismaying. It had been four days now and still no body. Poor Honey! She hoped the police would figure it out soon for Audrey's sake.

It was showtime. Stan, the bookstore owner, briefly introduced the authors as Kal and Karen Karloff. A tall, blonde, pale couple dressed in black stood up and went to the podium. Maryvonne thought they looked startlingly like a pair of vampires.

Kal thanked Stan, then began to speak, with a low and strange voice. His lips were an odd purplish color. Karen stood silently off to his side. Fierce eyebrows crowned her ice-blue eyes, which were penetrating the assembled crowd. Maryvonne glanced over at Zeus, who gave her hand a quick squeeze of mock fright. Maryvonne plastered a fake, frozen smile on her face and held her breath as the program began.

In his strange Vincent-Price-like voice, Kal listed the five haunted places that they had confirmed in Exeter in their work over the past year: The Parks and Rec building on Court Street, the small, brick chapel at the Exeter Cemetery, the Coffin House on Portsmouth Ave, the Nathaniel Gilman House on Front Street, and the Robinson House on Salem Street. These were all detailed in their new book.

Kal decreed bombastically that he would discuss two locations only. And he would not be taking any questions. He stated that his two discussions would both follow this outline: First he would state the lore of the place; second, he would summarize some of his final observations; third, if you wanted to know more, you would have to purchase the book. Karen then held up the book, like a haunted Vanna White, and glared at the audience some more.

This schtick was not like any author event Maryvonne had ever attended before. Apparently, this was the well-known modus operandum of the vampirish Karloff twins, and people ate it up. The pair travelled the country doing this, and were often featured on television. To each his own.

Kal Karloff asked the crowd which two they would like to hear about. Zeus and many others raised their hands. Kal pointed slowly at two people with his long, pale Grim-Reaper-like fingers. The Coffin House and the Robinson House were chosen. Zeus looked disappointed and lowered his hand.

"Ah, you have selected two homes with a common thread of Black history, very interesting choices." He crossed his arms and stepped back for a moment while Karen produced an ornate briefcase, unlocked it with a skeleton key and placed two yellowed, paper scrolls and two black folders on the table. She then resumed glaring at the audience.

Rather loudly Kal announced, "Now we begin: When Karen and I researched the Coffin House on Portsmouth Ave, this is the true story that we pieced together." He picked up one of the black folders and placed it in front of him on the podium.

Kal continued, the words flowing from his thin, purplish lips, his strange voice like the creaking of a door, "This current house was built over an earlier house, which was indeed more of a shack. The shack was owned by a Black man, Benjamin Jacob Paul, or Ben Jakes, as he was more commonly known. Ben had split with his wife, and had two children with another woman. This small house was the humble abode of this family of four: Ben, Betsey, and the children Mary Ann and Parker. From our research we feel that another person wanted to purchase Ben's property, and build their own home on it."

Here Kal paused for dramatic effect, then continued, "To quote one of your ancestors: *'In every sense of the word, Ben Jakes was the strongest man in town.'* This is perhaps why they did what they did that fateful night in 1834."

Again, he paused for dramatic effect, while Karen continued to glare. You could have heard a pin drop in the room, everyone was so still.

Kal continued, the words flowing from his spellbinding, shiny lips, "Hear me now: Ben Jakes was disfavored in town. But Ben Jakes' property was in a favorable location on the approach to town."

Karen then handed him one of the old scrolls, which he slowly unrolled, while she once again glared at the audience. This time, Karen slowly rotated her head so her fierce gaze slithered in a wide swath across the room, sparing no one. People seemed to shrink in their seats.

Kal began anew, the words flowing from his two, wet, wormy lips, "This, from another of your ancestors, and I quote from your Exeter Newsletter:"

> ...a plan was laid to get rid of them. Ben kept a gun in his house, it was deemed prudent to get him out of the way; so, a warrant was obtained against him for some pretended breach of the peace, and he was locked up in jail. That night was dark as Erebus, when a large crowd of men and boys surrounded Ben's house, and after removing the family and their few household goods, soon demolished the house and levelled it to the ground. Ben was released from jail the next day, only to find himself without house or home. This was no doubt an offense for which the authors would have been liable to severe punishment, had the proper steps been taken to prosecute the case. But Ben was without money or friends, and so had no remedy. After a few months, he left town to return no more. He died many years since in Strafford County. His son, Parker, died in the New Hampshire State prison. This is the only case of a mob destroying a dwelling in our ancient town. The home of Marcus Coffin now stands on the spot.

Kal did a mic-drop with the scroll, and it landed on the floor. He crossed his arms, and looked disquietingly at the audience.

The audience sat shocked and chagrined by this account.

Now Karen handed Kal the electric blue probe, and he held it aloft, declaring: "With these instruments we concur the house is haunted by the ghost of the boy, Parker. The young boy suffered a severe shock that night when the mob pulled down his house. His spirit was crushed and died in the house that fateful night, although

86

his body lived on for another ten years, only to die, angry and alone, in prison. Our instruments have recorded his disregarded pleas to the mob."

He twisted his lips into a horrifying frown and a soft other-worldly voice wafted out, *"What have you done with my father? Where will we live? Why do you hate us?"*

The audience was rapt.

Kal's original hair-raising voice returned, "The thermal cameras have picked up the outline of a young boy, clinging onto a fishing rod. Dead fish are often inexplicably found in various parts of the house. These are a symbol of his clinging to his happy times in his house by the river, before the mob attack. He will not leave until reparations are made."

There was much murmuring from the audience while Kal handed the probe back to Karen, who replaced it carefully on the table.

Kal then turned, gripped the black podium with his knobby, spidery fingers, and cleared his throat. "Now for the second selection: the Robinson House on 77 Salem Street."

The audience settled down for another round of horror. Maryvonne wasn't sure she could take it, but Zeus was eating it up like a happy skeptic at a séance.

Kal stated again that he would follow this outline: First he would state the lore of the place; second, he would summarize some of his observations; and third if you wanted to know more, you would have to purchase the book. This man did not believe in the soft-sell. But maybe that is why they sold a lot of books.

"Now," Kal began officiously, as he opened the second folder. Maryvonne morbidly stared at his freakish lips. "Now, the Robinson House was owned by a favorite cousin of your famous Exeter-born-and-educated citizen, William Robinson, a very wealthy man who made his fortune in the cotton business in Augusta, Georgia in the 1830's and beyond. He died the week General Sherman arrived in Atlanta to begin his infamous, scorched-earth 'March to the Sea' in May 1864. Court records indicate that Robinson quickly called three men to his home one night to discuss changing his will; to cut out the portion he had allotted to Exeter Yankees, ten years prior, for a school in honor of his sister. According to court records, the decision to change the will was agreed upon that night, the men would write up the changes in the morning. But, alas, morning never came for William Robinson!" Kal thundered this last part for emphasis. The dumb-struck crowd jumped in their seats.

"William Robinson died that very night," Kal purred in a most gruesome manner. "So, the money did indeed come to Exeter. And you good Yankees founded the Robinson Female Seminary, just as he had instructed. However, this was much to the dismay of his wife's rich and powerful family who had long owned a plantation dynasty in Georgia. They tried to invalidate the will both during and after the Civil War. And lost both times."

Here he paused for dramatic effect, as Karen handed him the second scroll. The crowd sat, stricken.

Kal's skeletonish hands slowly opened the scroll as the audience held their collective breath. Then his voice rang out loudly.

"Now hear this: I read you this regret-filled quote, from Robinson's own hand in a letter to his brother Jeremiah, dated June of 1845. And I quote:"

Overproduction of cotton by slave labor is at the bottom of evil, and the difficulty is to change the particular description of labor from that of growing cotton to that of the different kinds of manufacturing.

Kal went on, derisively, "And William Robinson should know since we have his tax schedules here, and I quote:"

1850 – 13 slaves: 7 female and 6 male
1860 – 32 slaves: 16 female and 16 male (ages 1 year old to seventy years old)
1863 – 29 slaves

"If you are not familiar with historical dates, let me refresh you that 1863 was the year of the Emancipation Proclamation, 1864 was the year he died, and 1867 was the date your girls school began operating." Kal paused to let that sink in, in all its horrible sadness.

He started again, while the crowd squirmed, "And finally, back in 1853 your Robinson had bequeathed in his will to his wife, and I quote:"

...a negro woman named Maria, and her children.

Kal bellicosely thundered on, "But Robinson did not die until ten years after he wrote his will, so the Negro woman that was actually bequeathed to his wife was named Laura Williams... and all her children."

Kal concluded, throwing the scroll to the ground. Karen upped the wattage in her horrifying glare and spread in in wide swaths from the front of the room to the back.

In the audience there were several alumnae of the old Robinson's Female Seminary, which had existed for nearly one hundred years until the building became so decrepit, they abandoned it. The sad hulk was consumed in a fiery blaze in 1961. The endowment lives on, and now funds scholarships. The elderly alumnae seated in the audience looked confused.

Karen ceremoniously handed Kal the probe, and he held it aloft and cried loudly:

"With these instruments we observe the house is haunted by the ghost of William Robinson, who was actually murdered when he refused to change his will and cut out his beloved hometown. He now hides from his murderers in the attic of this Salem Street house, it feels a refuge to him. We have discerned his outline near the stained-glass window. His name is scrawled on an antique child's chair in the attic. He passes time by arranging and rearranging tea tins. He plays a form of hide-n-seek by turning off lights, or tapping people on the back. And finally, in regret he will crumple up and throw to the side things made of cotton, as if he cannot abide it, since he feels it the cause of his death."

The crowd was buzzing loudly. One of the alums began weeping loudly. Maryvonne didn't know what to make of it. Zeus was smirking.

With a flourishing bow, Kal announced the end of his session, thanked his audience graciously, and stated he would now sign books. Karen continued to silently glare.

Chapter 8

Love to Love You

"Zut alors, that was much too much," groaned Maryvonne out on the sidewalk, finally having escaped the bookstore. "I won't sleep soundly for a week; lock the attic, mon chéri."

"Are you serious? What a load of bunk! He deduces that Robinson was murdered because he found his name on a chair in the attic? That's a stretch. I can't believe he put that in print. It really is a world full of fake news," declared Zeus, who subscribed to a magazine entitled *Skeptical Inquirer*.

Maryvonne was still very much in a state of dismay from the harrowing scene. "There must be some kernel of truth in there. They seem to have done some real research; he did read those quotes. Those two were so petrifying; Igor and Sister of Igor. She can probably actually slay people with her eyes." Maryvonne closed her eyes and shook her head vigorously as if to dispel their bad energy.

She went on, "They were ghastly. Do you think it was all an act, or are they really like that at home? Can you imagine?" replied Maryvonne. The fresh air and warm sun were making her shoulders relax, finally.

Zeus put his arm around her and laughed, "So I guess you don't want to go see Joe Hill do his reading of his *Twentieth Century Ghosts* in the Ioka Condos Community Room & Micro-Theater?"

"No way," she practically screamed. "Both Joe Hill and his dad Stephen King are complete masters of horror, I can't read either of them. I've had enough horror, let's go up to the art show now and shake off the ectoplasm of the twins."

Crossing the street, they walked towards the large, brick town hall. The sizeable stone steps led up past huge white columns and into a very old and historic-looking double door. Passing the first floor, Maryvonne peeked in to see Ellen and her crew setting up hundreds of chairs for the finale at the end of the day.

Maryvonne and Zeus then walked up a long, twisted staircase to the second floor. The three-leveled staircase was so historic that it creaked on nearly every step. On the top landing, off to the side, were the filming offices of the town cable channel.

The door was ajar, and as she passed by Maryvonne noticed the cameraman that had filmed Honey's funeral. He was seated at a bank of computers, editing film clips.

Zeus and Maryvonne entered the art gallery, which was large and bright and new. She smiled to be surrounded by the colorful art, and away from the vampires. She loved art, and she loved her husband. And she especially loved enjoying both of them at the same time.

Folding chairs were lined up in arched rows in the center of the room, facing a podium, and the art panels fanned out around the rest of the room. Another author, Mark Cole, a psychiatrist who wrote a book entitled "*Frolicking Boomers*" had just finished up his talk, and people were getting up from the seats and chattering.

Zeus excused himself to go use the restroom, and Maryvonne started to look at some of the art, alone. Out of the corner of her eye, Maryvonne noticed the guy with the grey shoes and the black shoelaces in the center of the room. He was holding onto a chair while chatting with another attendee. She worked her way near to them, while pretending to be absorbed in the art panels.

An older man, wearing a purple track suit with reflective silver stripes, was in mid-conversation with him. "Fred, I don't agree. You heard what the author said, people have to age; they can't go on forever. A body just has to break down at some point. I say dat your 'one-hundred-year theory' is too pie-in-the-sky." The man used his fingers to make air quotes about the name of the theory. He had a thick Brooklyn accent and the pronounced "theory" like "teary."

Fred replied, laughing, "Look at you. I bet you are going to make a hundred and still be running around in that track suit. I would put money on it. At the very least, I will see you in my office next week."

"You bet Fred; you're the best shrink I ever had. I'll see you then, buddy." The two shook hands, and Fred left the gallery. Maryvonne felt another piece of that puzzle click into place. So, "Fred" was a counselor of some sort at Bubbling Brook retirement community.

Zeus returned from his absence, but she didn't want to mention "Fred" to him right now and spoil the cheery vibe. She would tell him later at home. The happy couple wandered hand-in-hand for another fifteen minutes looking at all the literary-themed art in the room.

Maryvonne's piece had been hung with another that depicted a scene from the same book, *Female Quixotism*. The whimsical rendering in bright pastel crayons portrayed the long-in-the-tooth protagonist, Dorcasina, in the act of trying to woo a younger man. Her eyesight is going and she applies makeup with a heavy hand by candlelight. Additionally, she piles her graying hair atop her head in two very tall cones, and drapes a small swoop of sheer cloth in between them. She then makes a grand entrance descending a staircase in this garish manner. The artist captured Dorcasina mid-stair, and Maryvonne chuckled and scoffed, "Femme absurde."

Another display panel was dedicated to the book *A Separate Peace* and featured a very large, dreamy watercolor of two boys standing up high on a large tree limb over a swimming hole. Maryvonne recognized Bill Childs standing in front of the piece holding a yellow tag. "Is this your work, Bill?" she inquired, for she could tell it was in his flowing style. She had two of his pieces in her own house.

"Yes, it is, Maryvonne, and it just got sold! The prep school just bought it to hang in their library."

"Bon! Good for you, Bill! It is really gorgeous," exclaimed Maryvonne while leaning in to look closer at his strokes. Bill had a way of creating simple, solid chunks of color that evoked a dreamy realism.

Bill went on, "The writer was an alum of the prep school and he set that classic story on the campus here in Exeter. Funny to think how that one small book has been read and studied around the world."

"Books do have an amazing power to inform and persuade, all while being entertaining. It's like a spoonful of sugar making the medicine go down," Maryvonne twinkled as Bill tacked the yellow "sold" tag alongside his painting.

Moving further around the *Separate Peace* area, Maryvonne and Zeus admired a black and white photograph of a dual marble staircase, and a plaster of Paris sculpture of a leg cast, done with strips of poignant passages of the classic coming-of-age story. One of the strips said, "*We had thought only of ourselves, of what Devon owed us, and we had taken all of that and much more. Today's hymn was*

95

'Dear Lord and Father of Mankind Forgive Us Our Foolish Ways.'"

The strips made Maryvonne think of poor Honey all wrapped up like a mummy, lost somewhere. She shook it off and moved to the next panel, which featured author Dan Brown and his many books. Her favorite piece in the Dan Brown section was a grade-school globe that hung like a mobile. It had different colored small tags pinned into the globe that followed the trail of each of his globe-trotting mysteries like *The DaVinci Code*. Small squares, that orbited the globe on invisible strings, showed the faces of some of the actors who had played Dan's popular characters in the movie versions.

She and Zeus got a kick out of flicking the mobile to watch Tom Hanks and others go into manic orbit around the world. "C'est trés bon!" she exclaimed.

Another prolific Exeter author, John Irving, had two panels worth of art submissions. Maryvonne and Zeus each picked out their favorite. Zeus liked a *Cider House Rules* oil painting of the workers cabin in the apple orchard, with a melancholy figure smoking a cigarette in the roof. Maryvonne enjoyed a large acrylic from *Prayer for Owen Meany*: a brilliant red dress on a dressmaker form. As she looked at it, she thought about her fabulous pair of Stuart Weitzman red peau de soie sling backs with the silver glitter heel. It would be a perfect match.

Maryvonne was proud of how well the Exeter artists had heeded the call last year. Art and literature had combined into a bountiful offering in the bright room. The room shone with artistic and literary radiance. Exeter citizens were truly an engaged bunch.

Maryvonne recognized scenes from so many books; an ice cream cone on the ground in front of the

Stillwell's Shop entitled "Middle-school Angst" made her laugh. A portrait of Charlie Pratt biting into an apple made her pensive. A clever sketch of Jimi Hendrix holding a guitar made from the title of a Sneeden poem, "Contrapunctus #2", encouraged her smile again, for she was a big Jimi fan. The panel for the *Incident at Exeter* UFO book was truly strange.

Under a wood burning of a sign that said "Harold's Place," Zeus checked his watch and said it was time for him to go to his next event about the war pilot.

He handed her the car keys, and gave her a kiss goodbye at the top of the stairs. She told him she adored him, as she had done every single day of their marriage, then waved goodbye as he creaked his way down the old staircase.

Maryvonne turned to go back into the art gallery, and saw the cameraman in his office again through the slit in the slightly ajar door.

She had about ten more minutes before her next author, so she could use that time to ask the cameraman if his funeral film showed anything strange. Maybe she could get a look at it.

Raising her hand to knock on the door, she realized there was someone standing directly behind it, arguing with the cameraman. They must be coming out any second. Maryvonne backed up so she would not get trampled.

"I have as much right to that van as you do, and when I've signed it out first, I am going to take it. You can bully me all you want," said a woman's voice from behind the door, angrily.

"Whatever, Amy. But if you steal that van out from under me ever again, you are going to regret it," came the menacing reply from further back in the room.

"Have you been skipping your anger management classes again, you turd?" came the reply from behind the door.

"I'll make you regret it…" A scraping of a chair, then the door whipped open and a young girl with short dark hair and large, owly glasses came quickly out and slammed it behind her. A very perturbed Amy brushed past Maryvonne and flew down the stairs.

Maryvonne stood in the hallway, glad for the forethought to back up and get out of Amy's way. She watched the defiant girl race to the bottom of the stairs in record time.

Maryvonne heard some footsteps behind her and turned to see her friend, Florence, who had just left the gallery, and was heading into the hallway with a cheery, "Hello, Maryvonne!"

Maryvonne was glad to spend some time chatting with Florence, so things could cool down inside the TV office before she knocked on the door.

Florence, an older artist friend, had a copy of the *Frolicking Boomers* book tucked under her arm and commented to Maryvonne, "That author had some great tips in this book for having fun at my age. I am going to put on my rubber boots in the next spring rain and take a walk among the daffodils, and next fall I am definitely running through a big pile of fall leaves. You know, those four sugar maples on the lawn of the Congo church are spectacular every year, and I've always wanted to frolic in all that fiery orange, but was worried people would think I was odd at my age. But you know what? Who cares! I am going to frolic in nature every chance I get."

Florence tucked the book into her large purse and remarked, "I feel like a spring chicken anyway, since I moved to Bubbling Brook three years ago. There is something about that place that keeps a person young."

Maryvonne thought to the times she had frolicked in the colorful leaves with little Charlie, who vigorously enjoyed it. "You know what, Florence? I just might join you in those leaves next fall. That sounds like a blast! I'll bring my grandson; he loves diving into piles of crackling leaves."

"Definitely, wouldn't that be fun!" declared Florence, as she started slowly down the creaky staircase, all smiles.

Maryvonne turned and faced the office door and readied herself. It was all quiet from within, so she knocked on the door.

"Come in," was the curt reply. She opened the door and saw the cameraman alone at his banks of computers, rapidly working the computer mouse. She entered and stood awkwardly. He finally looked up at her, 'Can I help you?" he asked.

"Yes, hi, my name is Maryvonne," she began and stuck out her hand.

He got up, shook her hand and replied, "My name is Bert. Bert Mankiewicz."

"Hi, Bert. I am a friend, well, I was a friend, of Honey Lyman's and I noticed you were the cameraman at his funeral the other day." Bert narrowed his eyes as she said this, but he said nothing and just waited for her to continue.

She stammered, "Er, uh, I saw you up on the catwalk, and I thought you must have gotten a good view of the whole thing. Um, you see, Honey is still missing, and I thought that your tape may show something."

He was a tough customer. He just stood there, sussing her up with his narrowed eyes.

She continued, "Perhaps I could look at the tape? I might be able to see something that could help."

He answered, "I'm sorry, I gave the tape to the police. Now I got work to do, if you will excuse me," and he took hold of the door as if to hurry her out.

"Of course, you gave it to the police. Silly me. Well, thanks anyway, Bert. Let's hope the police find poor Honey soon. Thanks."

"Ya," he replied as he shut the door behind her.

The bum's rush! What was that all about? That guy *was* a turd. Maryvonne stood in the hall feeling awkward. Of course, the police would have wanted to look at the tape. Duh.

But wait. A tape? That was so 1980. Things were not filmed on "tape" anymore. That guy was more than a turd, he was a suspicious turd. "Étron du camera," Maryvonne sniffed under her breath, vexed by Bert.

A group of huffing women walked by her, out of breath from the long climb up the old staircase. From the hall, Maryvonne could see that most of the chairs were already taken in the gallery, and the next event was about to begin. Hurriedly, she sat herself in an empty chair just as Lara Morter was being introduced.

Lara had short brown hair, and big, round brown eyes. She was very gregarious and spoke about how her previous work as a private detective informed her writing. Lara had seen it all and knew nothing was too far-fetched.

100

She described her writing routine, and her writing aids. She was outspoken, informed, and engaging. Maryvonne loved it.

Lara began to talk about her latest book. She wrote mystery books that always involved cats in some way. And had a recipe. That was just Maryvonne's speed; not those vampire twins from this morning.

Lara did a quick reading from her book *Cat on a String Bridge* and then took many, many questions from the audience. It seemed to Maryvonne that there were quite a few budding authors in the room.

It occurred to Maryvonne that the LitFest was using current local writers to inspire future local writers: it was a sustainable loop. Maryvonne had to hand it to Ellen and her team, it was a great idea.

Lara's delightful talk was over, and Maryvonne got in line to buy a copy of her book and have it signed. After a small wait, she finally arrived at the table. Maryvonne told Lara that she had so enjoyed the talk, and was inspired to maybe try her hand at a mystery. Maryvonne then sighed, and said, "But I have no idea what I would ever write about."

But suddenly an idea did come to her. She dug around in her purse and pulled out the purple pill and showed it to Lara.

"Wait. I found this on the ground. Maybe I could write a mystery about this? Where would a sleuth go to get this tested to find out what it is?" she inquired.

"Well, I would work with the police, they have labs," replied Lara, eyeing the pill curiously.

"Hey, I can tell you what dat is," came a voice from behind her. It was the elderly man in the purple track suit. Maryvonne turned and held out the pill in her palm questioningly.

Scooping it out of her palm, the man looked at it closely and said "Yep, dat shade of purple is a dead giveaway. And it has the dot in the middle. And…"

He stopped and put his tongue to it, which caused both Maryvonne and Lara to emit a disgusted, "Ewww."

"And it tastes like it too. What you got here is a vitamin for the elderly. Try writin' a mystery around dat, ladies!" Maryvonne looked at him in wonder. It was as if "my cousin Vinnie" was now ninety years old and standing in front of her in a purple track suit.

He held out the pill to return it to her. Taking a tissue out of her purse, she wrapped it up while saying, "Thanks…I think?"

"No problem. Now it's my turn to get a book."

"Ok, I'll move along," she laughed, and said goodbye and thanks to Lara and "Vinnie."

Leaving the town hall, Maryvonne didn't want to pass by Bert's door again, so she took the elevator at the back of the room, and exited through the rear door.

Chapter 9

Heaven Must Have Sent You

Outside, Maryvonne went down the back hill behind the town hall and over towards the Salt Cave, which was the next location on her list. A spiritual author would talk about her new book, *In the Shade of Grandmother Willow*.

Maryvonne sat on a black metal bench out front of the Salt Cave, to relax before the next program. Alongside the bench was a small tree, whose swelling buds were jiggling in the spring breeze. Across the street the bookstore was all abustle. Absently-mindedly she began people-watching.

From both directions on the sidewalk people were streaming in and out of the busy bookstore. Maryvonne saw Ellen in the crowd, pulling a case of books along with a dolly. Ellen passed by a small, grey, wooden building in between the two tall and long brick blocks. As Ellen and her dolly passed under the wooden building's green sign engraved with "Martin Family Enterprises," it sunk in to Maryvonne that the building was John Cutler's old place. Hiding in plain sight!

"Très bien, there is one mystery solved," she said aloud to herself. "Alors, what about the ten others?" she sighed. She seemed to have only questions with no answers.

In the sun, since she finally had a minute to herself, she began to assess: Honey is missing, the purple pill is a vitamin, Bert's a suspicious turd, stories keep popping up about Exeter's old Black community, and Suffragettes in long skirts are talking to me. What does this all mean? She sat and pondered those things and more.

The Brim had been true to her word and had sent Maryvonne an email by the end of the day yesterday, with attachments of five or six 1907 obituaries of Ella

Follansby. Each one appeared in a different large city newspaper, from New Hampshire to Boston, and was written by a different judge, or politician, or trustee of an orphanage or hospital. They were all very long odes to Mrs. Follansby, and her tremendous accomplishments in the care of children.

They had read:

> *"Widely known through the state for her philanthropic work on behalf of children… protecting the orphan…very largely due to her unceasing efforts and influence that the law removing children from county alms-houses was passed…personally placed more than two hundred children…devoted much of her time and wealth to the comfort and education of young girls…had taken into her home more than thirty children…unassuming and unpretentious, her benefactions so sweetly and cordially bestowed…such faith in human nature…no woman in the state was held in higher esteem by men in high places…in her death the town and state have sustained a severe loss."*

Ella Follansby was a family-friendly rock star! She had been singularly effective at trying to change the world, one child at a time.

A breeze sauntered along the small sidewalk and got caught in the tree's budding branches. Maryvonne glanced up at the plump buds, shaking as if they were laughing.

She tried to focus on the Suffs' messages to her once again. Many of the rights Maryvonne enjoyed in today's world were due to their long struggle to have

105

women's voices heard. She was honored to have been chosen to bear witness.

Women had now been voting for one hundred years, almost exactly. What had changed? A whole lot. Maryvonne's Suffs would be thrilled at the world today.

But they would notice what parts didn't fulfill the promise of equality, too. What parts had been thwarted. And Ella would certainly notice how family health had been sacrificed in trying to pay the bills, or the race to keep up with the Joneses. Maryvonne leaned back and looked up into the blue sky. A sudden gust of wind shook the buds again.

Her ponderings were interrupted by a familiar voice, "M.V.! I thought I might see you at this talk!"

It was her Zen friend, Anjali. This small brunette was everything Maryvonne aspired to be: healthy, flexible, Zen, full of wisdom and love. A swear never passed her lips, cookies never rested on her hips, and she never gave unsolicited tips.

Maryvonne jumped up and hugged her friend. "It's so fantastique to see you, Anjali! Here, sit with me a moment before we go inside." The two friends sat on the bench.

"Heaven must have sent you. I was just knee-deep in thoughts, conundrums, and questions. Anjali, you always have a way of saying the most precise things. It's like you can look directly into the center of an onion without getting distracted by all the outside layers, but you still see how they all connect," Maryvonne observed.

"I appreciate your opinion of me, M.V., even if it is rather too high," replied Anjali.

"Modest and demure as usual, mon amie," grinned Maryvonne. "May I ask your thoughts on a matter of equality? To help me arrive at the pith quickly? No pressure."

"Of course. And I will give you as precise and pithy an answer as possible, since we only have ten minutes before the talk begins, and I want to get a good seat inside," replied Anjali, coyly.

Maryvonne took a deep breath while composing a succinct question from the loose rubble rattling around in her mind.

"Okay," Maryvonne began, "We seem to be in an era of reckoning. The landscape is changing under our feet, so people here are confused and frightened. Women, femmes and other LGBTQ's are refusing to be ignored anymore. Blacks and Native Tribes are refusing to be ignored anymore. There's a lack of equality." Maryvonne paused. "Are you following me so far?

Anjali nodded and said, "Yes, chickens have come home to roost, eons of silence have suddenly stopped, possibly due to widespread internet. Loudness prevails."

Maryvonne could feel Anjali's magic pith working on her, helping her to see the essence of the situation. "Yes!" she exclaimed, "Let's get to the center of the onion!"

Maryvonne then went on, "Okay now, since women got the vote in 1920, um, well that is not completely true in the case of Black women. Let me start over…"

Maryvonne paused to gather her disparate thoughts, then began again, "So, I have been reading up on Women's Suffrage. For many years prior to 1920, only about forty percent of men across the country voted YES when the question of whether women should vote appeared on their ballots. All the Suffs' speechifying and fasting did a little, but not enough, to persuade that remaining eleven percent of men. It was not until after women took their factory and industry jobs, while the men were away at war, that just enough men changed their mind to pass women's suffrage by the slimmest percent." Maryvonne stopped and looked to Anjali.

Anjali rejoined, "When women's rights and labor rights intersected, then things finally moved along. The option to work is good for women, on so many levels."

Maryvonne agreed with the synopsis and continued, "The option for women to work is best when the shape of it works for the entire family, and for people of every race. That's not been the case; children have suffered the brunt of it. The child has grown, but many have been hobbled, because children are outside the traditional equation of the economy."

Anjali offered the pith: "The current shape of labor can hobble children of all races. The equation is not balanced."

"Precisely," Maryvonne nodded and continued, "Now, a golden rule in life is that a small body overseeing a larger group should be made up of the same percentages as the group they represent, otherwise there is resentment."

"Yes, chickens will always come home to roost," smiled Anjali.

Maryvonne nodded. "Fifty percent of our population is female, and women vote in higher percentages than men do. Crawling at an inch-by-inch pace over the last one hundred years, women now make up less than thirty percent of our leadership; I'm talking congress, governors, state legislators. Blacks make up about thirteen percent of all citizens, and are in the same boat as far as leadership levels."

Anjali distilled Maryvonne's words to their essence: "Still thwarted. Something's gotta give."

Maryvonne nodded and smiled, "Today seems to be that day. Feels like we are in the death throes of an old order. The shape of the old thing doesn't fit anymore. People are spilling out all in the streets about everything. Now, I see the foundation of it all as compassion, or the lack of it, towards people and nature. People do not want an uncompassionate world anymore. Compassion is taught at home, but it's so hard to practice in a dog-eat-dog world. The family unit needs help. We need a big upgrade on healthcare, childcare, parent care, work schedules and more. The family needs to be stabilized to be able to engender compassion to all its members. See? This is where the whole thing intersects for me. I know the paths cross, but I don't know how it ties together best on a practical level. There are so many working parts."

After a minute, Anjali delivered the final pith: "The option for women to work is good. Compassion needs to thrive in the family. Loudness prevails. The equation is unbalanced. Bottom line: we need a shape that satisfies."

"A shape that satisfies. Hmm What is that shape?" asked Maryvonne, rather rhetorically.

"Balance," replied Anjali.

"What do you mean?" said Maryvonne, flummoxed.

"Balance the equation: If we balance the leadership, and balance the workplace, then we will balance families of all sorts and compassion will thrive," answered Anjali.

109

"What do you mean by 'balance the workplace?' By the percentages of gender and race?" Maryvonne was still barely following Anjali's pithy logic.

"No. I mean the mainstream shape of the labor schedule does not fit the family in its various forms and needs. The only hours considered serious are weekdays nine to five, or forty to sixty hours, and that shape is just not family-friendly. A schedule like that does not account for the infant, the child at school, the elder parents, the ill. Many times it dead-ends and suppresses compassion and creativity. A new shape is needed," Anjali replied, cupping her hands in the air in front of her, as if presenting a gift.

"I can't imagine what the shape should be," mused Maryvonne as she looked into Anjali's empty, cupped hands.

"The shape should be like this tree right here," Anjali answered, uncupping her hands and pointing to the small tree by the bench.

"What? I don't get it," Maryvonne looked at the tree in confusion.

"As above, so below: A large trunk, with many branching options on both ends." replied Anjali.

Maryvonne looked at her questioningly. Anjali continued, "This is a dwarf sugar maple; a perfect example of balance. The large round canopy at the top is balanced by an equal amount of roots underground."

Maryvonne could picture this, and she agreed, but still felt perplexed. She looked up at the tree again, its buds dancing in the slight breeze.

Anjali continued, "It doesn't have an outside leadership trying to make it fit some other schedule or job. The sweet sap only runs between the spring and fall equinoxes, then it stops. It is in perfect balance with the seasons; it buds in the spring, it glows like a fiery sunset in the fall, and rests in the winter. This sugar maple transmutes sun into shade, carbon dioxide into oxygen. It is in synch with nature. It is nature."

Then Anjali leaned in towards Maryvonne for the final encapsulation, "Roosting chickens clamor for compassion. We need a shape that satisfies. The thwart will be extinct very soon. Are you ready?"

Maryvonne was befuddled at first. But slowly the simple genius of it dawned on her.

In her soul, the burden of gender and race and super-woman expectation seemed to lighten a smidgen, both for herself and for future children of the world. Maryvonne covered her face with her hands for a moment and almost wept. The gleaning of a truth had its miraculous effect.

Maryvonne took her hands from her face, sat up, raised her eyes to the tree buds and said, "As above, so below. Of course!"

Anjali just sat and smiled like Buddha under the bodhi tree.

"Anjali - merci, merci, merci beaucoup! Inspiring! You don't need to go to the spiritual author's talk; you should give the talk," Maryvonne pronounced with a heart-deep gratefulness.

"You're welcome, M.V., now let's get in there and find a seat near those glowing salt walls. I do so love to be inside the Salt Cave. You know, this is my friend Kathy Brown's first book, and I want to cheer her on."

"Allons!" Maryvonne cried out joyfully, and together the two friends entered the glowing magical cave of wonders.

111

A small, silky feather, in the same shade as Ella Follansby's butter-colored ensemble, fell from the budding tree by the empty bench, and skipped merrily away on the spring breeze.

Chapter 10

Ring My Bell

After the author talk in the Salt Cave was over, Maryvonne had returned home for lunch with Zeus. As they were finishing up the hearty soup he had made, she told him about seeing Fred and "Vinnie," and that the purple pill was purported to be a vitamin for the elderly. She asked him what he made of it.

"Well, that seems pretty benign," he answered while dipping some of his home-made crusty bread into the hot soup.

"It does seem benign, so why does Fred pick it covertly off the side of a train? That makes no sense to me," she answered in between slurps of soup.

"What does it matter to you? You found out it's a vitamin for the elderly. Just leave it at that."

"I don't think it's a vitamin. Why is a shrink giving out vitamins to residents? I think it is contraband coming in from Boston," she said, half-jokingly.

Zeus looked at her. "Illegal drugs? Narcotics? Hallucinogenic? Experimental cancer pills? If that is the case, then you stay far, far, away. Maybe you should pass that purple pill on to the police, and rid yourself of the whole thing. Let them run tests or watch the train station, and when he picks up his next shipment, then they can ring his bell."

"Mon chéri, that is what I will do. I've so many other things to do rather than worry about this silly pill in my purse. I'll stop by the police station this afternoon. I think I will skip the afternoon segments of the LitFest. I may go out and sketch again for a bit, and then head over to see the four o'clock LitFest finale in the town hall."

Zeus looked exceedingly pleased with her reply. "Thanks, my dear, you have made me a very happy man."

~~~

At the police station, Maryvonne requested to see Officer Bailey Barndollar again. The fit, young woman entered the small conference room with a warm greeting. Maryvonne asked how the case was going with Honey.

"We're following some leads, but it's pretty slow," was all she would say.

"Did you see anything in the film the cameraman made?" Maryvonne questioned politely.

"There was someone filming?" asked the officer leaning in, very alert.

"The Clives didn't mention it? Yes, I saw Bert the cameraman up in the rear catwalk during Honey's final journey. I bumped into Bert in the town hall film studio this morning, and he said he gave you the tape," Maryvonne offered. Officer Bailey jotted some notes.

"Old Clive is not as sharp as he used to be, he probably forgot it in all the confusion. CJ didn't mention it either. I'll check into it," replied the officer, nonchalantly.

"I hope it helps, but that is not why I came. I came to give you this little purple pill," she said as she put the tissue containing the licked pill on the table. Office Bailey looked very surprised, and jotted more notes as Maryvonne described the entire odd story, beginning with the train platform and ending with the lick.

Maryvonne ended sheepishly with, "I'm sure it is nothing, but I'd rather leave it to you to decide. I hope the story doesn't seem too foolish to you. But it was bothering me, so I watched the guy. Sorry, for being a busy-body."

"Sometimes citizens give us our best tips, so don't worry about it at all. Thanks for telling me the story. We'll get this pill analyzed and take it from there."

Officer Bailey escorted Maryvonne through the maze of offices to the front door, and they said their goodbyes.

~~~

Maryvonne parked at the train station, got out, and looked around. She wanted to sketch the curtain factory from a different angle this time. Her head was feeling almost back to normal from the glue accident, so she knew time was running out.

Walking by the large public notice board near the train platform she noticed the glass door was unlocked and open, and a man was posting up a new schedule. It was Bob Hall, also known around town as "the train guy." Bob had been instrumental in the train's returning to Exeter after an absence of almost forty years. Today the Amtrak Downeaster stopped eight times a day in Exeter during the weekdays, serving about two hundred passengers daily.

"Hi Bob, how are you?" called out Maryvonne. He was just closing the glass door as he looked up to see her.

"Just fine, Maryvonne, nice day," he said as he locked the case and came over to her for a chat. He wore a new pair of blue mesh running sneakers. "It's so nice to get outside again."

"Yes, finally the weather is turning," she replied looking past him and noticing that the door was wide open on the old baggage house. This small, stone house at the depot had sat unused as long as she could remember. "Hey- what's going on in there?" she inquired.

"Well, you probably saw in the papers that the old variety store was recently bought. The baggage house was

116

part of the deal. The old depot and old baggage house are on the same lot. Both built in 1891 at the heyday. Handsome buildings, I remember when they were open way back when I was a young boy." Bob was a humble man who happened to have a true love of railroads.

"Yes, I did see that. The new owners are keeping the old breakfast diner going in the back of the shop. People are happy about that."

"Yes. And the new owners are fixing up the old baggage house. The stones are good on the outside, but the inside didn't make the grade. The floor was all rotted through and needs a total replacement. Who knows what they could find under that floor? They are going to revamp the place into a commissary kitchen for the restaurant."

"Good news. I'm happy to see the place get a new life. But it's fun to think about all the baggage and people that came through that tiny building since the 1890's. I wonder if they'll find any coins or jewels under the floor?"

Off in the distance they heard a long whistle. "Here she comes, right on time!" exclaimed Bob, getting side-tracked from the baggage house. "You know, a train makes different noises with its air-horn to signal different things."

"I didn't know, Bob. Can you speak train?" she asked playfully.

"Yes, that signal we just heard means the train is approaching a crossing. Listen; it's one long, again one long, then just before it gets to the street it's one short. Then when it is actually on the street it's the final long blast. So, it's: long, long, short, long. Then we'll hear the bell ring when it's pulling into the station; ding, ding, ding, ding. Then when passengers are all aboard and it is ready

117

to leave, it will give one long blast – that's called "whistling off" in the trade."

"I never noticed that!" exclaimed Maryvonne.

They watched as the 1:27 rounded the corner and came into view. The silver and blue Amtrak train came whooshing and clanking and hissing into the Exeter Train Station platform and the conductor put down the bridge and stepped out. A few passengers came out; then he called "All aboard!" and a few passengers got in. It was the same every time.

The conductor waved his hat to Bob, who took off his own ball cap and waved it back. Then, sure enough, the train gave one long blast and whistled off north.

Bob scratched his shiny head and watched the train rumble smoothly away. Then he turned to Maryvonne and said, "I saw you at the Heavenly Depot. I don't know about you, but I had quite a shock when the casket exploded. I wasn't sure if Honey was setting us all up for one last laugh, but now it sure doesn't seem it. Poor guy, I wonder what happened to him?"

"I wish I knew too. His poor niece Audrey is pretty rattled. I hope the police close the case soon," replied Maryvonne, shifting her art gear to the other arm.

Bob looked at her gear, "The sooner it's solved, the better. May Honey rest in peace, so people can get back on track with their lives. Speaking of that; you look like you're going to do some sketching. Are you drawing the train station?

"No, the Curtain Factory, though I may get a bit of the train station in the background."

Bob put his cap back on his head and said, "You might want to sketch the old Heavenly Depot at some point soon. I just heard a rumor that Old Clive and CJ are going to sell out, finally. That old building has had it, and the train station could use some more parking."

"Interesting," replied Maryvonne. "But his gardens are really nice; I wouldn't like to see them paved over. That faux-turntable is iconic. It's a town treasure."

"Old Clive sold the real stones from the turntable to a guy up on High Street, across from the hospital entrance, about thirty years ago. They're now a retaining wall. So, you never know how something old could end up being something new. Stranger things have happened." Bob was one optimistic guy with good karma, and Maryvonne smiled in agreement.

"Nice to talk to you, Maryvonne, and enjoy your art afternoon. I'll catch you later, got some more errands to do today," said Bob, putting his hands in his coat pocket, fishing for his keys, and walking to his car.

Alone now, Maryvonne scoped out the area, looking for a good spot to set up on. She knew there was not another train scheduled for hours, so she would be undisturbed in her task.

She spied the rear brick patio of a small coffee shop. It had a good view, but a young couple was seated there. Not good. Instead, Maryvonne looked past that spot and down the hill. She decided to set up in a secluded grassy spot below the coffee shop's patio and near the large porch of a red ramshackle barn.

She walked down the small hill and stood beside a scrubby bush. She could see the lower portion of the Curtain Factory, with a view of the train station beyond it.

Settling in, she looked up at the sound of a fast car approaching and saw Audrey's boyfriend, Richard, furiously driving down the slope next to her, looking very upset. He was scouring the Curtain Factory building with his eyes, and did not turn to see Maryvonne seated opposite, near the bush. He exited the back of the parking lot and sped off. Audrey was nowhere to be seen.

Odd. Maybe they were in a fight? But Audrey had said she was going to stay away from the shop for a few days and it seemed like the shop was closed. Why would Richard be there?

Maryvonne started to settle in again, when she saw a delivery van pull into the rear parking lot, and back up to the delivery door of one of the tangle of small buildings stuck to the Curtain Factory's rear flank.

On the van's side was painted "Remnant Palace/Odd Lots." A man in canvas overalls jumped out, opened the rear door of his van, and pushed a doorbell by the steel double-doors of the remnants room.

Maryvonne had been shopping in that room before. The customer access was from inside the building. After you made your way through the maze of displays, and down a small set of stairs, you would come to the large room at the rear. It was like a candy shop to those who loved fabric. It was filled with oversized wooden racks, more like bins really, into which were piled random six- and eight-foot bolts of upholstery and curtain fabric.

There were mountains of bolts, and not stored in any order that Maryvonne could discern. There were damasks and jacquards mixed in with ducks and moleskins. There were percales and poplins mixed in with chiffons and organdies. There were seersuckers and tartans mixed with moleskins and velvets and chenilles. In short, it was a smorgasbord of delights for fabric appreciators. In addition, there were bins of colored cord, tassels, and other trimmings for pillows and curtains. Maryvonne could be lost in there for hours looking at all the fabrics, patterns, and colors.

The delivery man was checking his cell phone while he waited for someone to answer the doorbell. No one came. He rang again, and after a minute he rang yet again. Still no one came. He then pulled on the handle of the door several times, but it was locked. Turning in exasperation, he slammed the rear door of his van shut and climbed back in the cab. He appeared to be on the phone for a minute talking, then he started the van and drove off, exiting the rear of the parking lot.

Finally, Maryvonne was alone. She had prepared her art space while watching the delivery man in his failed delivery attempt. Her sketch pad and pencils were in position. She had decided how she was going to render the building on paper. The purple earbuds were in her ears.

She took a minute to ground herself. Taking a deep breath, she held it and searched inside her skull for the indistinct borders. She ended by trying to focus on a point called the third eye, and pretend that she was slowly breathing through it. Her shoulders began to relax, as did her head. Her head felt like it was resting, balanced on her neck in perfect alignment.

Maryvonne let out a long sigh, hit play and the music washed over her brain like a warm bath. Tiny skyrockets kept time for the chicken scratch, punctuated by small bells like those on a bicycle handle. The jaunty rhythm rolled on until the smooth, whispery voice of Anita Ward slipped in:

> *I'm glad you're home*
> *Now did you really miss me?*
> *I guess you did by the look in your eye*

Maryvonne smiled and thought of Zeus and the look in his eyes at certain moments. She twisted her hips a couple of times as the back-up singers joined in with:

Look in your eye…
Look in your eye...

And she turned her full attention to the task. Her hands started moving across a blank page in her Strathmore sketchbook. The paper had a certain tooth to it that pulled back in a pleasing way, but not too much.

The task of blocking in was first, to ensure the proportions stayed tight. Foreground: a few branches of the budding bush. Midground: the rear of the dove gray building with a small pell-mell spattering of doors, small windows and porches. Background: the swoop of the hilly driveway with a suggestion of the train platform far in the distance.

The backup singers were cooing:

Ring it,
ring it,
ring it, ring it, ahhh!

Now to focus on the midground. The slant of the roof, the shading of the eaves. Those cute, white French-looking millwork medallions running around the top of the building under the eaves on the frieze board. It must have been a special place once-upon-a-time, too bad it was in such disrepair. A few small windows. An odd porch-like structure with no stairs. A crumbling parking lot.

Maryvonne's pencil was gliding across the page to the ethereal, striding beat of *Fly, Robin, Fly*. The song was so soaring and free. The violins took hold of her mind, like Peter Pan holding out his hand to Wendy at the window's edge.

Fly, Robin, fly...

The scraggly grass pressing up through cracks to plaster itself against the decrepit building, reaching ever-higher. A few puffy white clouds looked down on the building. Her mind poised on the window ledge.

Up, up to the sky...

And the slight shudder of the spangle as she slipped free, backwards and expanding, with a flash of light.

Chapter 11

Don't Leave Me This Way

The spangle intensified, quavered, then levelled off and as the diaphanous fog cleared, Maryvonne became aware of a ripple of women's laughter behind her. Behind her?

She turned and saw that the large porch of the old red barn behind her was filled with women in long skirts. They seemed to be cleaning up the remnants of a festive gathering. Both on the porch and on the lawn near the porch, folding chairs were slapping shut, china was clinking in stacks, and picnic baskets were being filled with leftover sweets.

Women carrying baskets, chairs, and other items were dispersing in all directions. A motor car packed with chairs was pulling away.

Two women with baskets on their arms passed close by to Maryvonne on their way home. She heard the older one say, "Oh Maybelle, it was so very nice to see Edith, even if only for an hour or two on her way to Portland. What a lovely gathering in her honor, and then whoosh – she is off on the next train."

The younger Maybelle replied, "Mrs. Wiggins was my favorite teacher at Robinson's Seminary. Of course, that was back when she was Miss Edith and taught art. She would absolutely adore the new painting that was sent from Madame Borgereaux in France last month and is to hang in the school."

"Ah, yes, I knew Madame Borgereaux from her childhood days in Exeter; she did lovely drawings even back then. Her canvas of "Crossing the Brook" is divine."

Maybelle stopped for a moment to re-arrange her heavy basket. "You know, I just heard that two more teachers got married and had to leave their jobs. Pity that schools go through teachers so fast. Students barely get to know so many of them and then they are off and married."

The two resumed walking away. "We'll that's the way of the world, dear," replied the older one; "women have got to stay home and take care of the husband and children. It's only natural."

"Is it? I'm beginning to wonder," replied Maybelle. They were getting far away and Maryvonne could no longer hear their conversation because a small group of three young girls were now passing her.

"Did you see the Hutchinson Family Singers get off the train when Miss Edith did? It's so exciting!" said one.

"Are they scheduled at the Opera House for after the current minstrel? That *Won't' You Come Home, Bill Bailey* show? I hope so, just to even out things; those weird black grease-paint faces make me cringe," said another. "My grandmother told me that Exeter used to have a big community of colored folks. I think now it's just Mrs. Walker's family and one other that haven't moved off to Boston or some other larger city. I don't think this town has been too good to colored folks like them over the years."

"Well, what does that matter? They can live where they want. Now, I heard that the Exeter Opera House is going to show a moving-picture next month. Can you imagine? Pictures that actually move? That will just be the end-all," said the third, all agog.

The three were walking very quickly out of earshot, so Maryvonne looked back at the stragglers left on the porch.

The six or so lingerers included her "Golden Girls"! The small group had pulled a few of the remaining

127

chairs into a circle and were engrossed in conversation. After the motor car with the chairs left, the area became quiet, and Maryvonne could hear them clearly.

"Ella is feeling poorly, and sent her regrets to Edith. Poor dear, something seems off with her," said Kate.

"Oh really?" replied Dr. Alice, looking a bit concerned.

"Yes. While Ella will never tell you directly, I can read the signs. My work desk is in the tower section on the front of my house. Hers is the same set up, across the street. I used to see her quite often working at her desk in the round room. But she doesn't' spend much time in there anymore. She appeared very weary over the winter. The warm weather earlier in the week pepped her up, but it seems she had a setback just now," said Kate.

Dr. Alice replied in her commanding voice, "I was going to tell her the news today, that after only three months of operation, the big orphan's home she helped found has cared for one hundred and fifty-seven children. She'll be happy to hear that, so I'll stop by tell her. Then I'll see if she wants me to take a look at her health," Dr. Alice said.

"Goodness gracious, I have six children, somedays it feels like one-hundred and fifty-six, and I get so weary too," chimed in a dark-skinned woman with a squirmy four-year-old boy on her lap. She pulled a small cookie out of one of her skirt pockets and passed it to him saying, "There now, Phillip, just one more minute please, then we'll get going home."

"Mother, let me hold him for a minute before I have to go back to work," said a demure dark-skinned teenaged girl who looked the image of her mother.

128

Rebecca passed him over to her, "There you go Ethel, thank you." Rebecca turned her attention back to the ladies, "He's getting antsy now, but at least he was behaved enough for me to visit with some of my old teachers. That's more than I expected. He's been a good boy today." She patted him endearingly on his little curly black head. "He's my last for sure. I got married when I was only fourteen and I've had six children. Since Frank abandoned us, I got a divorce and the constant pregnancy has ended. But it sure is busy at my house; sometimes I get so tired."

"Mrs. Walker, I don't know how you do it all. I'd be happy to watch your little ones now and again so you can have a break," said Annie, kindly. "And if you would like me to take Isabel out for a walk sometimes, I would love to do that. She is such a sweet girl."

"Thanks Annie, I may do that," she replied, adding, "Please call me Rebecca. We're doing all right, my little family, despite my foolish complaining. I just got some money from the Kate Holland Fund so Isabel can go to the Perkins School for the Blind in Boston. Every little bit helps. I just thank my lucky stars that the little ones still have me and don't have to go to an orphanage."

Dr. Alice broke in, "Though, in my opinion, there need not be so many orphans if pregnant girls would be helped to keep their children if they wanted. And believe me, the majority do. The hypocrisy is undeniable. It's all well and good to purport to 'save' the reputation of the woman – though we both know there always is a man involved too – but it's the poor child that pays the price so that the parents can remain in 'good standing' in society. It's unconscionable, unnatural, and it's going to come back to haunt this country someday." Dr. Alice stopped and shook her head.

She lowered her robust voice, then continued, "You all know about our scheming to work around this social morass and help girls keep their babies and give them a fresh start in a new town. But that only goes so far. We're only two people in one town, and this happens all over the country. Good Lord, do we need the vote!" she ended in exasperation.

Annie spoke up, "Well, the vote in town was almost fifty-fifty, so it can't be that far off, right?"

Dr. Alice replied, "Not the case. Let me get this note I wrote down." She fiddled around her long skirts looking for the pocket in all the folds, and then boomed out, "Darn skirt is like a shroud; this fabric is always hiding what I need." Finally, she pulled out a slip of paper and announced: "The State voted 14,162 for and 21,788 against!"

At these dim statistics Kate exclaimed, "Oh, what a slog it has been already, and only this far," she wrung her hands in dismay. "I remember when Mrs. Nutter, the minister's wife, became vice-president of the New Hampshire Women's Suffrage Association here back in 1855. It's been fifty years in the asking, and I fear it will be another fifty. The men are terrified of any hint of petticoat rule. They talk about the so-called 'ignorant vote', but there are just as many ignorant men as women in my observation, and besides, all can certainly be taught." Kate closed her eyes and shook her head.

Then Kate addressed the three girls in their late teens sitting in the circle with them, "Ethel, Olivia, Clarice, - you must all promise to continue the fight after we are all dead and gone; they can't thwart us forever."

Clarice, who looked a bit of a tomboy, put her hands behind her head and leaned back. "I've just started this fight," she said, then kicked her feet out in front of her and crossed her ankles casually. Her skirt was shorter than the others, and this exposed her bloomers and shoes. Suddenly, Maryvonne noticed all their shoes at once, for she was a shoe freak at heart.

The group all wore dark boots with curved Edwardian heels that laced up to mid-calf or so, although the tops could not be seen because of the long skirts, excepting Clarice. Clarice wore a more casual short Chelsea-style boot, with elastic panels on the sides and no laces. She didn't seem the type to want to fiddle with laces. Maryvonne saw clearly that she was the Louisa May Alcott of the group.

Clarice had leaned back even further until she was practically prone in the flimsy chair, "They're not gonna know what hit 'em when we get through. All the girls over at the Fellowes Box Shop, on both shifts, are signing on now. Even the ones who weren't sure before the men voted last week. I guess they just thought they could sit back and it would happen without their help. But the defeat has shocked them into action."

Clarice stood up dramatically, thrust one finger into the air, and emoted, "When old Templeton wrote his one line rebuttal in the paper yesterday of Mrs. Blatch's speech..." and here Clarice mocked him by pretending to twirl a mustache while speaking in a deep tone, " '...*Mrs. Blatch's tirade against the women of New Hampshire amounts to nothing more than a bad temper.*' Well by golly, he got the bad temper of a whole lot of women and girls all fired up. In the end we might thank him, because as I see it, all the girls are signing on to Suffrage now like a wildfire. And

131

they are even calling themselves Suffragettes; they are owning that word like a boss!" Clarice ended her monologue and clapped at her own performance.

Dr. Alice nodded enthusiastically, "I agree with Clarice, the cat is out of the bag now. I bet the NHWSA membership will double this year. Kate, I think you will get to cast your vote sooner than you think. Let's make a vow that when that day finally comes, we all go cast our vote together."

"I'll bring my elderly Aunt Lydia, she has vowed to live to one hundred so that she may finally cast her vote," said Annie.

"We'll be there, too!" cried Clarice, "But now we have to get back to work. Come on, Ethel, Olivia, I'll race you across the tracks!"

"Heavens, no!" declared the two other girls in unison as Ethel passed little Phillip back to her mother.

Olivia said, "Go on without us, and sign us back in, please. We'll be right behind you."

"As you wish," said Clarice, already starting up the small, curving driveway towards the tracks. Olivia and Ethel said their goodbyes and followed at a brisk pace while pinning their hats back on.

Clarice was a fast one, and Maryvonne saw her jumping across the rails like a deer, her hair falling loose out of her bun as she did, and she headed for the small brick factory opposite the train platform.

Her sudden movement scared a couple of hoboes hiding in the bushes on the far side of the tracks, and they scattered in alarm.

"Look at her go!" cried Alice, "She scatters men in her wake already; just wait until she grows up." Dr. Alice threw back her head and laughed heartily. "Okay girls, let's

132

get the rest of these chairs in the back of my motor car. I'll drive them back to Robinson's school, back up to the door, throw them in the storage bins, and be on my way."

They all stood up and took two chairs each over to the car. Kate suddenly spoke up, "Oh! Don't let me forget my package in the front seat. I bought a few yards of Georgette and some honey-colored silk to sew new curtains for my front hall."

Kate went to the passenger door and reached in to retrieve a soft package wrapped in brown paper and tied with strings. "Just where I left it, all wrapped up tight."

Maryvonne's heart skipped a beat. Georgette and silk? Yes! Bins and shrouds! That was it! She knew exactly where to look to find Honey and wrap up the mystery.

Dr. Alice started the motor car with a roar, and the scene tingled in a flash of light, and faded.

Maryvonne, sketchpad on her knee, stared into the empty parking lot for about three seconds. "Of course!" she yelled out loud as the sketchbook fell into the grass.

~~~

She knew it. She knew it to her bones where Honey was. Hurriedly, she jammed all the art supplies back into the bag, folded her stool. Grabbed her purse and took off towards her car.

Gear stowed safely in the car; she went to the front door of the Curtain Factory. A handwritten sign in black marker that said, "Closed for the weekend, death in the family" was taped to the glass. She peered in. It was very dark, for the building did not have a lot of windows towards the back.

133

Maryvonne returned to her car and got the folding stool. During her sketching she had noticed a small, strange porch with no steps hanging off the back of the building, about four feet off the ground. She had also noticed that there was a small window on this porch that was slightly open.

Standing at the back of the building, her eyes scanned this way and that to see if anyone was around, but the rear lot was vacant. Setting her folding stool up under the little porch, she saw that it would work.

She threw her purse up on the porch and stepped up on the small stool, using her hand on the wall as a brace. The stool was pretty wobbly. One hand reached out to the porch, and the other stayed on the wall. Then she got both hands on the porch, and with all her might she jumped skyward.

Success! Her hips settled firmly on the landing of the porch, and she was able to throw one leg up, then the other, and then scramble to a seated position. It wasn't pretty, but she had made it. She stood up and inspected the window. It was old and had cast iron windows weights dangling on the inside.

She took hold of the crusty wood, with its many layers of peeling paint, and struggled to push the window open enough to allow her to slip through. She slid her purse in and dropped it on the floor just inside the window. Then she went in head first. It was a tight squeeze. "Bof, too many eclairs," she said as she dangled by her hips, stuck for a moment.

Finally, she was in. That had not been pretty either. Not like the forever young Nancy Drew or the sleek Phryne Fisher, always investigating in high heels. But

134

Maryvonne was in, and she was not bleeding. She took that as success.

Dusting herself off, and fixing her blouse, she looked around. It seemed that she was in an employee breakroom.

There was an abandoned teacup, half full of tea, on the small table, along with some letters and a notebook. Maryvonne glanced at the return address on the outside of the large manilla envelope and saw that it was from a prestigious law firm in Portsmouth. She was as curious as a cat to find out what was inside, but that was not her mission so she passed by and headed to the door.

The door opened into the fabric cutting room. Bright sunlight splashed into the room from the many windows, but the darkened area beyond that was where she was determined to go. Digging around in her purse, she took out a small keychain LED flashlight. She surveyed the darkened room once more, and pursed her lips. Fishing some more in her purse, she came up with a mini pocket-knife, too.

She set her purse on the cutting table while she opened the blade, just in case. Purse hitched high on her shoulder, she put the micro-flashlight in one hand, and the open knife in the other. The flashlight was the annoying kind where you had to keep holding the button down for the light to work.

She pushed the button firmly, and stepped into the darkened area beyond the fabric cutting room. This was the part of the building that held many display couches and faux walls and faux windows. It was a maze in the light, and a trap in the dark. She shone the tiny beam of the flashlight on the wall by the door, looking for a light switch. After a fruitless search, she couldn't find one.

The building was old and had been added onto so many times, it was hard to find an actual wall, let alone find the switch. Added to that were the myriad displays swirling around in all directions, with large swatches of sample cloth hanging by each one. It was a like a fabric forest.

The tiny beam shone into the darkness, not reaching very far at all. Maryvonne knew she was going to get disoriented, and did not want to go in circles. How could she mark her trail?

She stood in the quiet, brainstorming possibilities, then discarding them. The building creaked, causing her to glance around in the dim corners. So many corners. Suddenly her mind went back to the Karloff vampire twins and she involuntarily shivered. Did she just hear a swish of fabric? Her hand gripped tighter around the tiny pocket-knife.

Mice. Yes, it could be mice. She was sure the decrepit building must be host to several families, at least.

Brainstorming again, she hit upon the idea of leaving a trail of throw pillows. Every couch display had two to four pillows on it, depending if it was a full-sized couch or a love seat. That could work. She stepped forward to the first display and reached for a pillow.

The problem here was that both of her hands were full; one with the knife, the other with the flashlight button. She made an executive decision that the hand with the knife was more important, and she would use the flashlight hand to grab the pillows.

But, as she put the first pillow on the floor behind her, she realized that to get a firm grip on the pillow meant she couldn't press hard enough on the flat button to keep the tiny beam lit.

In a halting fashion she went from pillow to pillow. Light on, she walked slowly to the next couch. Light off when she picked up the pillow and put it on the floor behind her. Light on, walk slowly to the next couch. Light off, a stiff cotton pillow under her fingers. Light on, walk slowly. Light off, a smooth satin pillow under her fingers. Light on. Light off. Her other hand clenched on the knife; because no matter how much she tried to talk herself out of it, she was getting more creeped out by the minute.

Some of the couches faced her, some faced away or at other angles. The darkened air smelled cloistered and dusty, like an attic, but with a hint of fabric dye. She thought of William Robinson's ghost, lounging on a couch in the dark. Shudder. Light on, light off. Light on, light off. She thought she might be halfway to the back of the building now.

She heard that swish of fabric again, only much louder this time. She let go of the flashlight button and stood still in the inky blackness. Her ears strained to pick up any noise.

She heard breathing. Did she hear breathing? No. Get a grip. If Zeus could see her now, he would be falling on the floor laughing. She raised a determined chin and carried on. Light on, light off. Light on, light off.

Now she could see a faint glimmer of daylight at the back. She was headed in the right direction. Light on, she stepped carefully to the next couch display. This couch faced away from her. Light off, she pulled the pillow up and a scream split the dark, heavy air. Maryvonne bolted and half jumped, half tripped over a big couch in the opposite direction. She crouched down behind it and

137

gripped the knife so hard that she cut her finger and gasped out loud.

Where was the flashlight? She had lost it in the escape. But that didn't matter. She heard something or someone scrambling in the dark. Peeking up over the top of her couch, she could see a faint outline of a person heading towards the sliver of daylight in the back.

Suddenly the figure tripped over something in the dark and hit the floor, hard. Maryvonne heard a woman say "Bloody hell" in a slightly English accent.

Maryvonne yelled out "Audrey? Audrey! It's Maryvonne."

Suddenly a light snapped on and flooded the rear displays. Audrey stood there, hand to her nose, which was bleeding. Like a prairie dog, Maryvonne peeked her head up again over the couch she was hiding behind.

"Crikey! Maryvonne! What are you doing here?" Audrey said, gulping to catch her breath while blood dripped through her fingers and onto her shirt.

"Are you hurt? Mon Dieu! Let me help you." Maryvonne scurried quickly to the back of the room where Audrey stood dripping. "Let me look," she said as she raised her hand, and then saw that it was dripping with blood too, from the pocket knife cut.

Audrey looked at Maryvonne's dripping hand for moment, and then began to laugh. Realizing the absurdity of the moment too, Maryvonne joined in.

Audrey looked around and picked two thick cotton fabric samples off the wall next to her. She gave one to Maryvonne, and placed the other under her bloody nose. The two stood for a few moments trying to staunch the flow of their respective wounds.

With her head tipped way back and a fresh fabric swatch under her nose, Audrey said, "I was dead asleep on my favorite couch when you pulled that pillow out from under me. I had no idea what was going on. Good God my heart almost stopped. What on earth are you doing in here? How did you get in?"

"I came in through the breakroom window. Sorry, I didn't think anyone was in here. I didn't mean to scare you. Actually, you scared me half to death too. And then I stabbed my own self. That didn't help."

"Why do you have a knife?" Audrey asked, her voice muffled through the bloody cloth.

"You have to admit it is kind of creepy in this old place."

"Creepy? I don't think so at all. I like the thought of ghosts. I feel like this place has many women lurking around in it, it feels so comforting to me. That's why I wanted to spend one last weekend here, alone, in their company," replied Audrey, muffled.

"I think Richard is looking for you, I saw his car outside a while ago."

"Probably. I needed to get my head straight, and I wanted to make my own decisions. It's been a shocking week. Now, what are you doing in here?" she demanded.

"Well, I have a hunch. More than a hunch. Since you like ghosts, let me tell you a secret. And please never say a word. It'll always be our secret. Okay?" pleaded Maryvonne.

Audrey tipped her head back down and checked the blood flow. It seemed to have stopped. She took the cloth away and stood with her head slightly tipped back, face still smeared with blood.

"That looks better, I think it stopped now," said Maryvonne, inspecting her. "Don't move about much, give it another minute or two."

Audrey tilted her head slightly back and said over her nose to Maryvonne, "I thought you were just being a curtain-twitcher. But it's more sinister than that? Ghosts, secrets; sounds interesting."

"It's a sorry fact that I'm rather nosy; I like to think of it as curious or adventurous myself. But that's not why I broke in here. Audrey, you may or may not believe this, but I've gotten a message of sorts telling me the whereabouts of your uncle."

Audrey's head came forward in surprise. "Tilt your head back, Audrey, or you might bleed again. It's a long story… but I think Honey is in the lower room."

Audrey put her head forward again, then caught herself and tilted it backwards again and said, "In the remnants room?" she asked, looking down her nose.

"Yes. Let's go see. I'll lead you there after I pick up my purse." Maryvonne retrieved her scattered purse from behind the couch. The pocket knife was still open, so she closed it carefully, vowing to never again arm herself with a knife. She was her own worst enemy and would surely end up on the wrong side of the blade again.

Walking back to Audrey, she took hold of her with her unbloodied hand. "Keep your head tilted back while we walk," she advised.

Maryvonne led her further back in the room. They went through a twist and a turn, down a small staircase and into the remnants room. Audrey, head still tilted back, found the light switch, which was secreted behind a box of cherry-colored piping cord, and flipped it on.

A riot of colors appeared. In all directions. The remnants room was actually two rooms that joined in an L-shape. Old wooden bins and shelves held mountains of bolts, but Maryvonne passed by most of them and went directly to the rear delivery door area with its tiny, reinforced window. Audrey followed slowly, looking down her nose with her tipped head back.

With her non-bloody hand, Maryvonne began pushing bolts around in the bin until she spied what she was looking for. "Aha! Here's a stack of Georgette fabric bolts. Let's see what's underneath." The sheer, gauzy fabric was hard to keep rolled and kept flowing everywhere.

Finally, the golden silk in the shape of a mummy was exposed. Maryvonne leaned over and said, "Hello, Honey, did you think I would leave you this way, my old friend?"

Audrey stood by with her mouth gaping. Finally, she said, "Dear Lord in Heaven, it is Uncle Honey!" and the shock of it caused her nose to bleed again, which she didn't even notice as she stood there dazed.

A loud knock on the delivery door startled the wits out of both of them. The two were still drenched in adrenaline.

They could see Officer Bailey Barndollar's face peering through the tiny glass window. Maryvonne unlocked the bolts and opened the door.

Officer Bailey looked at Maryvonne's hand, wrapped in a bloody swatch, and then looked over at Audrey's bloody nose, chin and shirt and she stopped in mid hello.

"Is everything all right here?" the officer asked, looking apprehensive.

141

"Quite," replied Audrey jubilantly, "we just found my uncle!"

"I see. I thought the body might be in here. But, why are you both bleeding?" asked the officer calmly.

"We tripped over a couch, I can be pretty uncoordinated sometimes," replied Maryvonne, quickly.

"I see," replied the officer, dubiously. "And how did you happen to come across the body just now?"

Audrey replied, now wiping her nose with a fresh piece of cloth, "I'm doing a special-order job for Maryvonne, and we came back here to look at the fabrics, and, well, there he was. Quite a shock, really."

Maryvonne felt a whoosh of relief course through her at Audrey's answer.

Officer Bailey turned to look at Maryvonne with interest. "Maryvonne, aren't you always in the right place at the right time, somehow?" Maryvonne just looked at her innocently and smiled her biggest cat smile.

The officer went on, "Your tip about Bert the cameraman panned out. He confessed that he put the body in the back of his van, and then hid it here in the remnants room the morning after the funeral."

Maryvonne exclaimed, "He confessed!? Waouh!" She couldn't believe it. Maryvonne then added, "But why did he take Honey in the first place? Did he have something against him?"

"Not against him; against Jeff Reed. Seems Bert was playing a bad joke on Jeff, and it went awry. I'll tell you about it later, after I file the official report. Right now, I've got to call into the station. We'll send your uncle back over to the Heavenly Depot soon, Audrey."

Audrey replied, "Thank you! Thank you! What a relief to have closure! Oh… now I am bleeding again." She pressed the bloody cloth to her face. "Officer, please excuse me while I go to the breakroom and wash my face. Please do come up and get us if you need anything else. But let us get out of the way now, while you police do your thing."

The policewoman nodded, then attended to her squawking walkie talkie as the two bloodied women went back up the small stairs.

Chapter 12

Last Dance

Maryvonne and Audrey returned to the scene of their mishap in the couch display area. Droplets of blood were splattered randomly on the huge, old hardwood floor of the former bowling alley and bicycle training arena.

Maryvonne looked down guiltily and assessed the situation. "Let's come back and clean this later. First, we need to wash your face, it does look rather alarming, and get you some ibuprofen to ward off any swelling. I'm so sorry about all this blood, Audrey."

"You also have a streak of blood on your face, I'm not sure if it is yours or mine," Audrey laughed.

The blood-stained pair continued walking until they got to the next section of the capacious room. Audrey slid her hand behind a faux window that was nailed to the wall and flipped a switch. The room lit up, and Maryvonne's trail of pillows came into view.

Audrey turned to Maryvonne with a questioning look. "I didn't have any breadcrumbs," confessed Maryvonne, slightly abashed. "Don't worry, I'll put them back right after we get washed up. I don't want to touch anything now with my bloody hands."

They walked on to the next darkened room, and Audrey reached behind a faux potted fern and flipped that light on, chuckling at the next pillow trail. Soon they were in the breakroom. Audrey picked up a small backpack and pulled a clean shirt from it, then went into a tiny bathroom off to the side.

Alone now, Maryvonne felt an intense sense of relief that Honey was finally found. She went over to the kitchenette sink and washed her hands slowly. The cut on her finger was not too deep, and was starting to clot already. She carefully washed around it, then wrapped a clean paper towel around it and looked around for some tape on the desk.

Audrey finally came out of the bathroom with a fresh face and a glass of water. She fetched a bottle of pills out of her purse and swallowed two. "Much better, but I think I should lie down for a bit to make sure this nose has fully stopped."

Maryvonne picked up the roll of paper towels, a plastic bag, and a spray bottle of cleaner then escorted Audrey back to the couch display area.

Audrey lay back on the first full-size couch they came upon. Maryvonne handed her a few paper towels, and said she would be right back after replacing all the pillows and wiping up the blood off the wooden floor.

As Maryvonne scrubbed the floor, she thought of the Golden Girls and women of their era, and how they had taken bicycle lessons in this building. Bicycles were an avatar for Suffragettes, allowing women a new level of freedom of movement. Women of all sorts, on bikes, dreaming of freedom and equality; that made Maryvonne smile as she scrubbed.

It occurred to Maryvonne as she inspected her work, that she was standing on the actual footsteps of those fighting women who won the right to vote for her.

Team Suff had won the rights back then, and now one-hundred years later - thwarts-be-gone - today's women were finally on the cusp of actually claiming their full share of the power conferred in those rights. And that was good news for families and a national family-friendly economy.

The fact that the old building had not been updated much was actually good, because the original flooring had remained. In fact, the more Maryvonne thought about it, the more she began to realize the old building was a town treasure.

A knowing suddenly dawned on Maryvonne; it was her turn now. But instead of Team Suff, it was Team Fam. Or whatever it was going to be called by historians. The twin concepts of family-friendly workplaces, along with a decoupling of health insurance from the employer, were two of the missing pieces that would protect women and their families. This would relieve the pressure on parents, children, and employers – and that would promote compassion in the world at large.

Ella's phrase "So much work to do, and so little time," instantly popped into her head and Maryvonne wasn't sure if she was thinking about family protections or the cleaning up of the blood. She walked around the big couch she had tripped over in the dark and checked the floor there. More blood to clean up, on the back of the couch and the floor.

As she sprayed and scrubbed, she thought that maybe that scratched, old wooden floor was part of the charm for Audrey; why she felt such a kinship to the building. Maryvonne was beginning to feel the same.

Her thoughts drifted back to Audrey on the couch. Poor thing must be in shock, finding her uncle in a bin at the back of her shop. Stuffing all the dirty paper towels into the plastic bag, she returned to Audrey's side and sat down on a small couch near her to inquire how she was doing.

"I'm feeling much better now," Audrey said, sitting up tentatively, while keeping her head somewhat tilted back. Is it all cleaned up?"

"Yes, pretty spic and span. Although I can't guarantee that you won't find a random drop of blood here or there on some fabric," replied Maryvonne.

"That's fine. I'm going to close the shop anyway."

"For the rest of the week?" asked Maryvonne.

"No, forever. Well at least the majority of it."

"What are you talking about, Audrey, are you moving away now that your uncle is gone?"

"Maryvonne, that's why I closed the shop and holed up inside for the past twenty-four hours. I had a lot of thinking to do, and I spent all night last night working out a plan in the breakroom. I worked myself to complete exhaustion. That's why I was fast asleep on my favorite couch when you yanked that pillow out from under me." They both laughed at the tom-foolery of the pillow affair.

Audrey went on, "Uncle Honey was the conductor of a gravy train. It came as a big surprise to me how much money Uncle Honey left me in his will. A shock really. Well, another shock; it's been a radical few days, Maryvonne. But, thankfully, I have spoken with a therapist who really helped me to begin to see clearly." Audrey slowly tested putting her head in a more normal position, then continued to explain to Maryvonne.

"You see, I love this old building. I wanted to commune with the building alone, to really sit and meditate and have it speak to me. It has such a great history, and it has some good bones in parts of it. Other parts, not so much. But I can work with that. Now, thanks to Uncle Honey, I am going to pay off my loan and massively renovate this building into an affordable children's daycare center. A very big one. There's a huge need, you know."

149

Maryvonne was bowled over and cried out "Bon! Of course! That is so magnifique! Audrey, what a great idea."

Maryvonne stood up and did a little dance, "These old floors haven't seen their last dance yet. They are going to be so happy to have little children playing on them. And kids love to see that train go by – put some big windows on the train station side. This is going to be a very popular building."

Maryvonne had stopped dancing, looked thoughtfully around and added, "Again," as her eyes landed on a fabric swatch of donegal tweed.

Unexpectedly, Maryvonne realized she was near tears of joy at Audrey's news, for some reason she couldn't quite put her finger on.

"Not only that," Audrey went on, "but I am also going to ask Richard to marry me, I mean – if he is still interested."

That statement made tears of joy flow freely from both girls' eyes. "You'd better lie back down, you might start bleeding again," cautioned Maryvonne, warmly.

~~~

Two months later, Maryvonne and Zeus sat in their side garden on a green wooden swing under a grape arbor, reading the newspaper. The vines were freshly leafed out in the noontime sun that cast its dappled shadows on them as they gently swung back and forth. Honey Lyman was safely buried in the cemetery. Audrey had had a blow-out fabric sale, and then she and her fiancée had emptied the building. Construction had just gotten underway.

At the same time, demolition was completed at the Heavenly Depot, and CJ was a happy man... just about to take his early retirement. Old Clive finally sold, after twenty years of hanging on to the property.

Turned out that Old Clive and Honey had a bet: whoever died first would submit to having an epitaph, of the other's choosing, engraved on his headstone. Each Christmas, the two oldsters would terrorize each other with new epitaph possibilities written in their Christmas cards.

During the private graveside interment, Old Clive had listed some of them for the small gathering, as they said their final goodbyes to Honey.

"He was a ham" was countered one year with "He was side-tracked." Other years' contenders were: "Curtain-Called" versus "Undertakers never lie." "Still waiting in the wings" versus "Death laughed at him." And so on for twenty years.

The final winner was: "His was the greatest final scene ever." Somewhere in heaven, or hell, Honey was smiling.

Bert Mankiewicz was never charged with malfeasance. Both Jeff and Audrey, as well as Old Clive, agreed that Honey's last wish was granted beyond his wildest dreams.

True, Bert tried to play an awful and spiteful prank on Jeff Reed, against whom he held a grudge due to a production filming argument two years prior, but no real harm was done.

Bert had confessed to Office Bailey that he was on his way out of the restroom at the last minute, when he saw Jeff come out of the door of the private family room, shut the door quickly and furtively look both ways before going into the main room. Bert decided to look inside the room to see what Jeff was up to. It looked like Jeff had put the mummy on a gurney before pushing the "GO" button on the Casket Caboose and leaving the room.

Bert was not quite sure what Jeff was up to, but thinking rashly, he grabbed the gurney and rolled it quickly to the back door. Bert tucked the body under a pad in the back of his van, intending to embarrass Jeff. Bert figured it would make a great spoof film to capture Jeff's befuddlement and make a viral meme out of it to mock him.

What Bert didn't know was that Amy, though young, was nobody's peon. When she got to work and saw the van was gone, she decided to assert herself and take the van to her out-of-town assignment anyway, despite Bert's bullying. She went over to the Heavenly Depot and hijacked the company van. Amy didn't notice the mummy in the darkened rear, so was none the wiser when she dropped the van back at work early the next morning.

Enraged, Bert grabbed the van first thing in the morning and drove to the Heavenly Depot to secretly return the body. But the police were still on the scene, and he panicked.

He saw the rear door to the remnants room held ajar with a brick, so he backed up to the door and hid the body under some fabric bolts. He figured it would be found pretty quickly, and no one would suspect him. Maryvonne, though, did see him driving away that morning.

Officer Bailey Barndollar made Bert agree to attend anger management classes before he got himself in real trouble next time.

~~~

When Old Clive sold out, he emptied the building, had it razed to the bare ground, and split the lot in three. The gardens with the turntable he gifted to Audrey as a playground for the new daycare center. Old Clive would continue to care for the gardens, and watch the little children watching the trains, for as long as he was able.

The rest of the Heavenly Depot land was to be divided in half; the town would pave it over to make extra parking for the train station on one side, and a self-storage company had purchased the other side and intended to put up climate-controlled steel units. All the threads had been tied up except one, and now Maryvonne was on the swing hearing Zeus read the news article about it.

Zeus folded the paper and said "See, it's a good thing you turned that purple pill over to the police. They did their job splendidly. Slick Fred, your benign-looking counselor, is now awaiting trial for giving the unknowing elders at Bubbling Brook an unapproved experimental pill that purports to lengthen telomeres, the caps at the end of each strand of DNA, to stop aging."

"Yes, Audrey told me the police found a small baggie of those pills in Honey's apartment during their investigation. Fred claims he lost a small baggie last winter and has no idea how they showed up in Honey's apartment. Audrey had a talk with that guy I told you about in the purple track suit. He thinks maybe Honey was doubling up on them. But he swears it couldn't kill him, because it makes them all live longer."

"Have you ever heard of 'too much of a good thing?'" replied Zeus.

153

"Honey was in his nineties. I'm sure his was a natural death. The odds were getting slimmer every month for him. But Fred was trying to cheat those odds for himself by experimenting on his patients. What an imbecile. He deserves what is coming to him."

"And you just happened to be the one to see slick Fred pick his illegal pill delivery off the side of a train. Just happened to be the one. Why is that, Maryvonne? Why does trouble find *you* in particular?"

"You found me, too. So, are you saying you are trouble?" she countered.

He guffawed and looked at her with amused annoyance, "You are a piece of work, my love."

"You know I adore you, mon chéri," she quipped, lovingly.

They noticed a car pulling into the driveway, "There's Ellen now!" Maryvonne said breezily. She stood up and slipped her feet into the bronze Havaianas flip-flops she had kicked off into the grass. She was wearing shorts and a tee shirt over a bathing suit. It was going to be the first hot day of the season, and she and Ellen were going to take the Zeus-mobile, top down, to the beach.

Ellen came around to the side yard and passed through the arched gate in the white picket fence. "I've got the tuna – have you got the chips?" she whooped out as a greeting.

"Oui, oui, oui!" replied Maryvonne. "Let me run in the house and get my beach bag, be right back out." Maryvonne entered the house through the sliding glass door to gather her beach stuff.

Zeus put the newspaper down and stood up to greet Ellen. "Hello Ellen, long time no see. Last time was at the Litfest. But I do keep reading about you in the newspapers. You're organizing a memorial now?"

"Hi Zeus, good to see you. Thanks for sharing your wife today on this splendid beach day." She smiled and took off her sunglasses. "Yes, I'm doing some organizing to help the town create a small memorial heritage park in honor of the historic Black community that once lived here. We've got an ad-hoc group formed with reps from various town committees, trying to make sure we get it right. We're reviewing how the past two centuries of town conduct has delivered us to this singular moment, and how best Exeter should rise to receive it," she replied.

"Good for you; that's long overdue. Are you working on that Black community mapping project too?"

"No, that's another group from the high school. The kids are looking for all the homes, businesses, and the graves of the former Black community. So many things are unmarked. The community had basically vanished by 1910, so things have been brushed to the side for a long time."

"It's too bad there's no one left from the community to speak for it," mused Zeus.

"Sometimes I get verklempt thinking about the families and the discrimination they had to endure here. But, actually, in a way there are folks still around to speak for the old community. Slowly but surely, descendants of families like the Halls, Whitfields, Cutlers and Walkers are making themselves known to Exeter. And that's one of the main points of creating a memorial space; as a bridge of reckoning between yesterday and today."

Ellen looked down at the sunglasses in her hand and said, "Look at all the schmutz." She took a small cloth out of her pocket and started cleaning smudges off her

155

sunglasses while she continued, "The memorial space is meant for reckoning and healing."

"Thanks for helping to change the old narrative, Ellen. It's happening all over the country now, and New Hampshire is no exception," Zeus replied.

"It's turning out to be a great project. So many people helping and so many excellent outcomes. For example, for the LitFest finale each year we try to invite a descendant of that historic community to read some of James Monroe Whitfield's abolitionist poetry from the town hall stage. This year we had a woman who is the great, great, great grandniece of John G. Cutler, the famous hotelier," said Ellen, deciding the sunglasses were clean enough and pushing the cloth back into her pocket.

Maryvonne had returned halfway through this conversation, with her beach bag and an aluminum bottle of water. She cut in, "Yes, Zora was the girl Ellen and I had dinner with at Ron's Landing last month. You remember I told you? We all went to check out Rufus's old establishment. Zora is really interesting and fun."

Zeus commended her, "You sure are a busy woman, Ellen."

Maryvonne pulled her car keys out of her pocket, looked at Ellen and quipped, "You want something done – ask a busy woman."

Ellen chuckled, then said, "You ready, girlfriend?" and slipped on her clean sunglasses, with a sassy attitude.

"Mais oui," replied Maryvonne, taking her sunglasses out of her beach bag and slipping them on with equal sass. "Allons, to the convertible; let the beach season commence!" she said enthusiastically.

Zeus chortled, and as they rounded the corner of the house towards the driveway he called after them, "You two remind me of Thelma and Louise; don't get into any trouble at the beach."

Ellen had already rounded the corner, but Maryvonne turned back and took a few steps towards her husband.

"Mon chéri, there are two big differences between Thelma and Louise and Ellen and me."

He squinted at her standing happily in her shorts and flip-flops in the warm, bright sun and asked, "Oh, and what are they?"

"Number one: we are not seeking revenge, but seeking to heal."

"I see. And what's number two?"

Before she disappeared around the corner, she blew him a kiss and said, "I absolutely adore my husband."

**

Goddess Hot Chocolate
When you feel stone cold, this warms you

1 or 2 Tbsp Hershey's Powdered Cocoa (to taste)
1 or 2 Tbsp Stonyfield Vanilla Yogurt (it's thick)
1 or 2 Tbsp Honey and/or Molasses (to taste)
¼ teaspoon Coconut Oil
Hot Water

~In your goddess mug, vigorously blend the cocoa
and yogurt with a splash of warm water, until the
consistency of brownie batter. Add honey and/or
molasses and oil and mix until smooth. Then fill the
mug with very hot - but not boiling water - you don't
want to kill all the live goodies. Blend until creamy,
and enjoy.

*Naturally abundant in probiotics,
antioxidants & antivirals*

ABOUT THE AUTHOR

RM Allen is an artivist who spends most of her time in New Hampshire with her wonderful husband. She enjoys looking at shoes. More at RM-Allen.com

~~~

This book is part of a historical-fiction trilogy that explores the contributions of historical Black figures from Exeter, NH.

"Incident at Exeter Tavern" – Revolutionary War era
"Incident at Ioka" – Abolitionist era
"Incident at Exeter Depot" – Suffragette era

All book profits to be donated towards physical commemorations of Exeter's historic Black community.

Made in the USA
Middletown, DE
26 January 2022

59722529R00102